CW00517619

GOLDEN

HELEN JULIET

Golden
Copyright © 2021 by Helen Juliet

This book is a work of fiction. Names, places, and incidents are either products of the author's imagination or are used fictitiously. Any resemblance to actual events, locales, or persons, living or dead, is entirely coincidental.

All rights reserved. No part of this book may be used or reproduced in any manner whatsoever without written permission, except in the case of brief quotations embodied in critical articles and reviews.

GOLDIE

My hand trembles as I press on the buzzer for Honipot Productions. I step back and glance around the busy London street. All these people are rushing past me, and I can't help but wonder if any of them are hiding their gut-wrenching fear like I am.

What the hell am I going to do?

I'm going to go into this office building and see what Mr. Cundall has to offer me. That's what I'm going to do. I clutch at the satchel strap across my body and make myself breathe slowly and deeply.

"It's going to be okay," I whisper to myself as the door clicks, and I let myself into the dingy lobby. I pause a moment to hold the door for a bike messenger struggling past me with a large cardboard box, making sure he's out of earshot before I start babbling to myself again. "Any job he has to offer has *got* to pay more than the café. It'll be okay. You'll sort this all out."

No matter how much I say it as I travel up in the lift that smells of onions and sweat, I don't really believe myself.

How the bloody hell did I get myself into this situation?

Well, I know exactly how.

I gulp as the doors ping open, and I step out onto the threadbare carpet, looking for the right sign on the wall along the corridor. Honipot is a big company, or so I thought. I'd assumed their office would be somewhere fancy. I remind myself it's mean to judge a book by its cover and march over to the door I need, knocking as confidently as I can manage.

"Come in!" a man's voice barks, so I turn the slightly grimy door handle and enter the office.

There are two desks, both sporting old-looking computers, one to my left, the other in front of me, both facing my way, as I come to a stop in the middle of the room. To my left sits a frumpy middle-aged woman with a scowl, typing away. In front of me, a man with a comb-over rises to his feet, his arms open and a beaming smile on his face.

"There he is!" he cries. He claps his hands together and indicates the hard-looking chair in front of his desk. "Robert's friend."

I bristle as I take the seat whilst he perches on the edge of his desk, looking down at me. I try not to fidget, but his gaze is kind of all-encompassing.

"Robert's ex-boyfriend," I correct, hoping it's not going to fuck me over. But Robert is most certainly not my friend anymore. I doubt he ever really was. "Thank you for contacting me, Mr. Cundall. I'm so incredibly sorry about this whole situation and am eager to discuss any possibilities where I can sort it out quicker—"

He cuts me off by shaking his head and waving his hands. "These things happen. Let's not worry too much about how we got here, hmm? Let's think about the future!"

"Yes," I agree with a nod, my mouth dry.

I'd really rather not rehash how Robert used my credit history and generous nature to get a loan as an advance on royalties from Honipot, tied me into that loan—just me, not both of us like he'd told me—then completely blew everything on a project that never even got off the ground.

I owe the man in front of me thousands of pounds that will take me years to pay back.

He doesn't want to wait years.

I had no idea what else to do until he called me up yesterday and asked me to come in so I could discuss an employment opportunity with him that could help speed up the process considerably.

I jumped at the chance.

"So…do you want me to do filing or something?" I ask.

I'd done a lot of office temp work after I'd finished school, but with Mum's condition and all her appointments, a strict nine-to-five was never going to work for me. The café's pay is pretty bad, but it's around the corner from home, and my boss, Flora, is really decent about giving me flexible hours.

Mr. Cundall chuckles at my filing suggestion.

"I'm taking my break," the frowning woman announces in a grumbling voice before stomping out the door.

Leaving me alone with Mr. Cundall.

This is fine, I tell myself, sort of believing it.

"Do you know what we do here at Honipot?" Mr. Cundall asks with a smile like he's my caring uncle or something.

I swallow. I know exactly what they do, and I'm fine with it. In fact, I'm a fan. Or I was until Robert sullied it all.

"You're an adult film company specialising in entertainment for men who love men," I say, paraphrasing the spiel on their website.

Mr. Cundall clicks his fingers in a loud crack and winks at me. "Got it in one. Clever boy. And we do pretty all right for ourselves." He waves a hand dismissively. "Don't let this place fool you. I'm too cheap to pay for

3

anything better. I usually meet talent at fancy hotels and the like. It helps to go places where we also have private rooms when we need to see a demonstration, if you know what I mean."

He winks again, and my stomach flips, not in a good way. But I smile and laugh all the same.

"This place is nice," I lie. I'd rather clean the café's toilets all day than work in this drab hole, but he doesn't need to know that.

Mr. Cundall presses both his index fingers against his lips before speaking again. He looks concerned now, but this all feels like an act he's been rehearsing.

"I want to help you, son. I really do. I'm not a monster. It's obvious that this mess isn't your fault."

"Thank y—"

"But the loan *is* in your name," Mr. Cundall cuts me off, then tuts and shakes his head sadly. "So legally you *are* responsible for its repayment."

My mouth goes even drier than it was before. "I know," I rasp. "I know. I swear, Mr. Cundall, I'm saving every penny, but money's pretty tight and—"

He cuts me off again.

"I'm an impatient man," he says bluntly. "I need that money to fund other projects."

Not with Robert, I hope for everyone's sake. That man apparently can't organise a piss up in a brewery, not that I'm all that surprised. Our relationship was pretty disastrous. I only stayed with him so long because he kept saying he'd be lost without me, and I absolutely believed that. He could barely tie his shoes, for pity's sake.

I rub my damp palms on my jeans. "I-I can work here and the café," I stammer. Fuck knows who'll help Mum out, but I'll figure that out later. "I'll get a third job if I have to. I won't let your company suffer for Robert's mistake."

Mr. Cundall hums, then leans down...and touches my chin with his thumb and finger.

I stop breathing.

"You are *very* pretty," he murmurs.

I'm not a total fucking idiot. I know how the movie business has operated since its inception. I lick my lips and try not to faint from fear. "Thank you," I whisper.

"How would you like to work off your debt to me in front of the camera?"

I blink. That was *not* what I'd been expecting him to say. "I...uh..."

He leans back and nods, holding on to the desk instead of my face once more. That's a relief, at least.

"Here's my proposal," he says. "You work for free until those projects make back the total of the debt you owe me. You've got far too pretty a face to waste in an office like this."

I wonder if he means working in it...or letting him fuck me in it.

My insides rinse with repulsion at that idea. But what he's actually proposing...

"You want me to do porn for you? For free?" I ask.

He scoffs. "Don't make it sound so seedy!" he cries, flashing me that grin again. "You like sex, right? And you're a fan of our work? Robert said you were."

That was true. Mr. Cundall must have talked to Robert about me. The thought doesn't sit well with me. I can just imagine Robert thinking it was all quite funny that I now have to pay off this huge chunk of change.

Mr. Cundall winks. "So all I'm suggesting is that you lie back, think of England, and allow some seriously hot guys to fuck your brains out. I'll do the calculations, but I reckon it'll only take a few films and then—*poof*—you'll have earned me enough to repay your debt. What do you say?"

I lick my lips, hardly daring to breathe.

Because my first knee-jerk reaction is *excitement*. That sounds like it could be really hot, under the right circumstances. If I got to pick who I worked with and what kind of things we did.

But—wait—what the hell am I thinking?! I can't do *porn!* That will haunt me for the rest of my life! Won't it?

I chew my lower lip.

All the debt would be gone. I could just worry about myself and Mum again. No more ghost of Robert hanging over me. If all I'd have to do was be a pillow princess and lie there...how hard could that be, really? And it's not like I have any friends anymore who might be appalled, and I can't ever see myself having a fancy career that it would hinder. Mum would never accidentally see anything like that. If I do it under an alias...

I take a shaky breath and rub my chest. "Okay," I say before I can change my mind. "So long as I can approve which films I want to do before I book them, then...yes. I think that sounds like a good solution."

Mr. Cundall claps his hands, and I can practically see the pound signs in his eyes. I just think I'm a skinny twink with unruly hair, but he obviously sees differently. I get a flurry of goosebumps thinking about who he might be picturing me with already. Another young twink, both of us pretending to be virgins? A big, tough bloke bossing the shit out of me?

Wow, I guess I'm not as freaked out by this as I thought I might be. It just depends on the other guy.

A shiver of worry runs through me. If he's awful, I'll just say no.

If I *can* actually say no. I *have* to clear this debt before it eats me alive.

I know in that moment I'll do whatever it takes.

2

DADDY

THERE'S NOTHING BETTER ON A RANDOM TUESDAY EVENING than kicking back and watching my men fuck.

My dressing gown is open as I lounge comfortably naked in my armchair in the corner of the bedroom. One hand holds my whiskey. The other leisurely strokes my hard cock, not in any rush.

"That's it, Papa," I say, my voice low and full of promise and command. "Take our baby slowly. Tease him. Put on a show for Daddy."

Baby gasps and whimpers, reaching up to kiss his husband as Papa grinds him into the mattress. They're both panting and shining with perspiration, eagerly waiting for me to allow them to come.

I'll think about it. I'm *definitely* going to come soon. Maybe I'll fuck Papa whilst he comes inside Baby. Or maybe I'll make them crawl over here and get them to both suck me off. Even after all these years together, I still get high thinking about all the possibilities for how I can wring every last drop of pleasure from us all.

That's my job, and I'm bloody good at it.

What isn't a part of the plan is my phone ringing. I've got it next to me in case I felt like filming, but I had been enjoying my men all to myself for a change. I scowl at the caller ID—Cundall from Honipot—and tap the icon to send it to voicemail, dimming the bright screen. I never have my ringtone or notifications on, not even on vibrate. One, the damn thing would never stop chirping if I didn't, and two, we're always filming and that would ruin the take.

I glare at the phone to make sure it's dark, then return my attention back to the delicious sight, smells, and sounds of my men putting on a show for their Daddy. Papa has flipped Baby over onto his back with Baby's heels over his shoulders. Their eyes are lovingly locked as they gasp and grunt.

Should I let them come now?

Definitely not, as my fucking phone rings *again.*

"What in gay fucking *hell?*" I snap as I slam the device against my ear, placing my drink down on the small side table.

"Hey, mate!" Cundall, the shit, doesn't even sound contrite at interrupting my evening. "How's it hanging?"

"Hard and leaking," I growl, squeezing my cock tightly.

As furious as I am at the interruption, it's hot as hell that Papa hasn't stalled for one second as he drives Baby crazy beneath him. I told my men to fuck, so they're fucking. Nothing else—not even a call from our sleazy manager—is going to stop them.

"I have a new playmate for you," Cundall says, ignoring me. There's an annoying sing-song to his voice, but I can't say I share his enthusiasm.

"Another dumb gym bunny?" I ask with a sigh.

Sure, we'll take him in for a day or two and rock his world, but it's all got a little predictable. I'd rather make scorching hot content with just my men because viewers really can tell the difference. We can just jerk each other off and kiss and get twice as many views compared to a complicated scene with one or two other guys.

"Something a little different, actually," Cundall says, too smug for his own good.

I roll my eyes. "Do you have a file?"

When he says he does, I tell him to send it over, then hang on the line whilst I check it out. I smirk to myself as I put the call on speakerphone, subjecting our manager to some organic, unplanned fucking noises. He probably won't be unnerved, considering his line of business, but I like to think he's at least getting hard in that awful office of his as my men put on a show.

The slapping of skin and gnashing of teeth are my soundtrack as I navigate to my email, vaguely curious as I open the attachments.

Then everything else fades away as a golden-haired angel stares back at me through the screen. He's young—barely in his twenties, I'd guess—with gorgeous curls that fall around his ears, pale skin, wide blue eyes, and full bow-shaped lips that look like they were made for sweet smiles and sucking dick.

My breath hitches, and my flagging erection comes back full force as my balls tingle in anticipation. "I haven't seen him before," I comment, not magnanimous enough to let Cundall know he might actually *have* something here.

"He's brand new," our manager says, sounding even more smug, which means he knows I'm impressed anyway. The fucker. "I'm giving him a trial run with a few films to see if he can make me any money. I thought I'd give you guys first dibs as our biggest earners, then try him with a few of my other regulars—"

"*No,*" I bark, forceful enough that Papa's head snaps towards me and his thrusts slow. Good idea, actually. I crook my finger at them both. "Come here," I murmur.

9

They both wince and pant as Papa pulls out of Baby's arse. Their cocks are bright red and straining with need, but they come to me as commanded because my men are so good for me. My heart swells with pride.

Cundall does well for once and keeps his mouth shut as I show my men the selfie of the golden angel. "What do you think?" I ask. "Do you want to play with him?" I've already made my mind up, but I love my men and want to see their excitement, too. I have no doubt they'll feel the same.

Sure enough, their eyes light up as they take in the simple photo. He's completely different to all the guys we've fucked around with in the past few years. I think a change of pace could be just what the doctor ordered.

I hum, reminding them that I asked them a question, so they need to answer. I slip my hand around Baby's cock and my lips over Papa's leaking tip. They both jerk beautifully at my touch.

"He's gorgeous," Papa says reverently. "So sweet and innocent."

"I think we could show him a *really* good time," Baby agrees playfully.

"Get him tested," I instruct Cundall. "We'll have him bareback this weekend."

"Oh, well," Cundall says, immediately pissing me off. I told him what to do. Why is he sounding like he's going to question me? "The boy probably needs to work on a few films for me so I can see what he's like. I have a few other calls to make. Therefore—"

"Get him tested, and get him *here*," I growl dangerously. I squeeze Papa's cock hard, and he gasps. Baby kisses him over my head. They know I love it when we're all connected. "He's going to be ours and only ours over the entire weekend. Friday evening to Monday morning. Is that understood?"

Cundall makes a funny noise that I don't care to interpret.

"Yes, that should be plenty of time for him to earn…I mean, yes, I'll get it organised. Thank you. You won't regret—"

I close the call, already bored. I want the golden angel here right the fuck now. But until then, I have two gorgeous, strapping men at my command, and the first thing I'm going to do is get them to come all over my chest before I throw them back onto the bed and take my time fucking them both.

Like I'd share that pretty boy with *anyone* until I've had my fill of him. If he's new on the scene, I'm going to claim every inch of that beautiful, lithe body for myself and my men.

He is *mine.*

3

GOLDIE

WHEN MY PHONE STARTS RINGING IN THE MIDDLE OF THE greasy spoon café where I work, my heart almost jumps clean out of my chest. Luckily, I'd just brought some food out, so I wasn't carrying anything. Otherwise I have a feeling the plates would have gone flying.

My face is flaming as the old Spice Girls song blares through the place, mocking my attempts to retrieve the phone from my pocket and shut it up. I'm just about to hit the accept call button when I jerk my head up to search out my boss, Flora, standing at the till.

"I'm so sorry. It's about my mum," I say breathlessly. *Technically,* that's true.

"Yeah, sure, love," she says with a sad smile. She knows how awesome my mum is, but also how many appointments she needs to go to for her physio and the like.

I manage to answer just before the call from Honipot rings off. "Hello?" I say breathlessly as I make my way out the back door into the alleyway with the stinky bins.

"All right, superstar?" Mr. Cundall leers down the line and

I wince, safe in the knowledge that he can't see me. "Have I got some good news for you."

"Yeah?" My heart is racing, and my fingers are tingling. This is really happening.

Should I be excited or scared?

"Clear your weekend. From Friday evening until Monday morning, you are the proud property of a certain trio of tantalising men."

I frown and swallow, not quite understanding. A long weekend away from Mum? Who was he talking about? Three films, one after the other, maybe?

He sighs, sounding exasperated, and I bite my lip.

"Daddy, Papa, and Baby," he says in a clipped tone, like I've spoiled his fun by not immediately guessing.

I don't care. My whole world has just dropped through my cheap knock-off trainers right through the puddle-ridden concrete and has probably just bounced off the Hammersmith and City Line.

How could I have guessed that was what he'd been about to say, though? He might as well have announced that Prince James and his husband had invited me over for tea.

"I—you—*what?*"

"Thought you might be happy with that," Mr. Cundall gloats.

But I shake my head, feeling dizzy. Daddy, Papa, and Baby. My favourite adult entertainers. Only *the* most watched channel on all of Honipot's services. They have over two hundred thousand Twitter followers and over *three hundred thousand* Instagram followers. I don't even know about their Only Fans.

This is too much. Too big. I can't wrap my head around it.

"Um, that's great," I manage to croak. "But, uh, what are the other options?"

I can pretty much hear Mr. Cundall blinking down the

other end of the line. "What do you mean 'other options'? This is the *only* option! Didn't you hear what I said?"

I take a deep breath and put my hand on the brick wall to steady myself. It's gritty and wet under my fingertips, and the sensation helps me to focus.

"I did. Uh, it's just…a lot. I've never done anything like this before. I'm not—"

"No one's expecting you to do anything other than as you're told," Mr. Cundall snaps, making my hairs stand on end. "What aren't you getting? You're going to spend the weekend with my three hottest guys. Is that a problem?"

There is that scintillating excitement again, flurrying unbidden through my body. I briefly entertain the notion before reality comes crashing back down.

"You can't book me with them," I say in a small voice. "They'd never want me."

Again with the infuriating pause. "Pretty boy, I showed them your file, and they booked you. I don't know why this is so difficult to understand. Oh, you need to get tested right away, though. They want you bareback, and what they want, they get."

He makes a clicking noise with his tongue, then laughs, but I'm still stuck several sentences back.

"They want *me*? *Daddy* wants *me*?"

"No," he scoffs, and my heart drops.

Of course it was too good to be true. Someone like Daddy would never, ever be interested in a nobody like me. But then Mr. Cundall's voice cuts through my despair.

"He *demanded* he have you. Exclusively."

I don't have any words. My mouth just hangs open like a goldfish. "But *why?*" I eventually ask before I can have a stern word with myself about looking gift horses in their mouths.

Mr. Cundall snorts. "I mean, you are immensely fuckable. You must have noticed that? All that cherub hair and big blue eyes and bee-stung lips bollocks. I knew I wasn't going to have any trouble convincing guys to be interested in you. But ol' Daddy got positively feral at the idea of sharing you with anyone else. Therefore—this is the *only* job on offer."

My heart sinks again, powerful shame rushing through me. "So he knows about our, um, arrangement?" I don't want anyone knowing what I'm having to do to save myself and my mum from the repercussions of my ex's stupid, selfish mistakes.

"No," Mr. Cundall says impatiently. "That's bad for business. He just thinks you're fresh on the scene, and that's the way it's going to stay. He wants first dibs, like a dog with a juicy bone. So I take it that's a yes from you then? Come on, this isn't rocket science and I've got plenty else to be getting on with today."

I shake my head as if that might organise my thoughts. "He and Papa and Baby are *so* famous, though. What if I fuck up?"

"Fucking is all you have to do," Mr. Cundall says, laughing at his own bad joke.

And...so what if I fuck up and am no good? Mr. Cundall's right. I'll just have to do what Daddy tells me and...well, honestly? That sounds delicious. Terrifying, but also kind of delicious.

What do I really have to lose here? Nothing. But there's everything to gain. Freedom from this debt I never asked for, freedom from Robert. And...

Holy fucking bollocking bastard *shit.* Daddy really demanded me exclusively? I still don't understand why, but I'd be a monumental fucknut to pass up an opportunity like this just because I was scared of the unknown. I'm twenty-one and lived a very boring life. Almost everything is unknown to me. If I jump on this, then maybe *one* day in my far distant debt-free future someone maybe *might* care I was in a porno that one time.

Or not just once…

Now I've warmed to the idea that my favourite super-famous adult entertainers might be interested in me…do I want anyone else?

"So…after this weekend…" I hedge. But I think Mr. Cundall is really done with me.

"That's it," he snaps. *"Finito, fini, fertig!* I have no doubt that the revenue generated from this series of films will cover your debt, and your glittering career in the porn industry will be cut tragically short." He manages to wait a whole beat. "Unless you'd like to discuss—"

"Thank you *so* much, Mr. Cundall," I interrupt. It's one thing to agree to this moment of madness to pay my dues. I am absolutely not looking for a career change, however. Or even a career start. "This is incredible. I'll head over to Dean Street today after my shift and get thoroughly tested."

I know I don't need to. I've not been with anyone since I broke up with Robert, and I got tested then just in case he'd been cheating on me. But I'll do anything Daddy says. I wouldn't dream of pissing him off before we'd even met.

I close the call and stare at a stray banana peel on the ground for a while. This is really happening. Daddy, Papa, and Baby want *me.* I'm going to go spend a long weekend at their *house.*

What the fuck am I even going to wear?

4

GOLDIE

It's not like I've never left London before. But there's something entirely magical about the way the city falls away as the train speeds down the line and the countryside rises in its place. I feel like a little kid with my nose pressed to the glass as I leave Paddington and head west, my heart in my throat and my skin tingling with anticipation.

This is really happening.

Thankfully, the money I'd scrimped together to start paying Cundall back the loan was enough to cover the cost of a private nurse to pop in to look after Mum a few times whilst I'm gone, as well as for a proper deep-tissue massage from a therapist. I wouldn't have been okay leaving otherwise. This will be the longest I've ever been away from her.

She has good times and bad times with her multiple sclerosis—it'll relapse and come back without warning. Luckily, she's doing pretty great right now, but I would never forgive myself if she woke up in a bad way tomorrow all alone. With a couple of planned nurse visits as well as our neighbours on call in case of emergency, I can relax and focus on myself for once.

Or at least try and relax.

I realise I'm biting my thumbnail and make myself stop. It's a gross habit that I only do when I'm really wound up. Normally, it's because I'm anxious, and there's definitely a lot of that floating about inside me. But that tantalising excitement is also lurking again, making my heart race and my palms damp.

What the hell am I going to say when I meet them? Will they be like they are on camera? Daddy seems so fierce with Papa and Baby doting on him. It makes me shiver at how hot it would be to have that kind of relationship. Where someone is so confident that they just make all the tough decisions, not to mention take charge in the bedroom. I've never had a partner like that, but I've read a *lot* of gay romance books with Doms and Daddies, and the idea definitely gets me off.

A sharp stab of worry cuts through my excitement. Robert always used to say I was 'limp' in the bedroom. I think he wanted a more active partner, but I just get so shy and anxious during sex. What if Daddy and the others are disappointed in me? Their playmates always seem so lively and fun.

They're going to regret asking for me.

No, I tell myself sternly as I watch green fields speed past, broken up with twisty stone walls that have probably stood there for hundreds of years. Thinking about the people who made them calms me. They all had their own lives, their own struggles and hopes and achievements. I'm just a drop in the ocean, a speck in the universe. I am small and quiet and don't need to let these worries get any bigger than they already are.

Mr. Cundall was very clear that Daddy *demanded* to have me come stay with them. He's chosen silly little me for this honour, and it would be rude to turn it down or question it. I still don't really see *why* he's interested, but I'm trying my very best to count my blessings and not ruin such an amazing opportunity. Things like this just don't happen to me. At school, I was never the best at anything or popular, and I certainly never won anything. It was about time I hit the jackpot for something.

The biggest jackpot is obviously that my debt is going to be cleared. If I can manage to not fuck this up, I'll be about to earn enough for Mr. Cundall to forget all about this whole nasty loan business. But I do allow myself just the tiniest bit of pride that, for whatever reason, Daddy picked *me.* He wants *me.*

The train journey isn't too long—just under an hour and a half to get into Bath Spa. Then I'll need to take another train and a taxi to get to the house where Daddy, Papa, and Baby live together. I had to sign a non-disclosure agreement to promise that I wouldn't tell anyone else the address, which was kind of thrilling.

Most adult entertainers that I've seen live in fancy high-rise flats with spectacular views of cities all around the world. But Daddy and his partners are always posting photos on Instagram of them going for long walks down country lanes or drinking tea in their pretty back garden. I love that they include snippets of their lives like that, and it's not all about sex.

I feel like they must all really love each other.

The idea of polyamory seemed awful and stressful to me before. I couldn't imagine how the people involved wouldn't get jealous. But watching throuples like Daddy, Papa, and Baby made me realise that there are different kinds of love to go around, and it can be amazing to open your heart up like that.

Or so it seems online. I guess I'm going to find out what

it's like in reality soon enough. But after my last relationship with Robert (my only long-term relationship), I honestly can't imagine having just *one* nice boyfriend, let alone two.

I eat the sandwich I brought from home and continue to gaze out of the window, my thoughts swirling between nerves and anticipation. I want to read more of my book—a particularly sappy romance with hardly any angst—but after trying a couple of times to focus on the words that just keep swimming about on the screen, I give up.

Instead, I go through the next steps of my journey several times to make sure I won't get off at the wrong stop or anything. Then I use my phone camera as a reflection to try and tame some of my wild blond curls. As usual, they have no intention of cooperating, so I give up and start scrolling through Daddy, Papa, and Baby's Instagram instead. I'm not sure if it soothes me or riles me up, but I can't seem to stop.

As it's Insta, there's nothing too naughty on there, not like Twitter, where they can show *everything.* I haven't been brave enough to look on there again since Mr. Cundall's phone call on Tuesday. Even just thinking that in a few days there could very well be little videos of me naked on there makes me feel quivery. It's exciting but also very scary.

What if people think I'm no good?

I shift in my seat and have to bite my lip at the welcome distraction from my thoughts.

Getting tested at the clinic wasn't the *only* instruction Daddy gave me through Mr. Cundall. The other was that I arrive douched and stretched, ready for anything. So yesterday, I'd conquered my embarrassment and walked into an adult shop in Soho and bought my very first butt plug.

I have to admit there is something sensational about walking around with a kinky little secret like that. Nobody knows that I'm doing something *naughty.*

Except it doesn't feel naughty. It feels exhilarating to be

given an order and then follow it through. My heart flutters, and I can't help but daydream that Daddy will tell me I've been very good for him.

I want to be good so badly.

That's all that matters. Not what strangers on the internet might think. I just want Daddy to be happy with me. I don't want to disappoint him.

My little secret stays with me as I change trains in Bath and head down to Frome, getting off at a chocolate-box-pretty town called Trowbridge. As I exit the station, I find myself in front of a cute cream church. There are old pubs in renovated Tudor buildings and houses painted a variety of pastel colours, not to mention trees everywhere, their leaves turning as the season changes. Even the streetlamps are charming with their old-fashioned black wrought-iron style.

I breathe in deeply and close my eyes for a second, feeling calmer. It's so completely different to the never-ending hustle and bustle of London. I've always thought of myself as a city boy, probably because I've never known anything else. But perhaps I'm not. It's like the countryside is already plucking my worries from me and letting them drift away in the autumn breeze.

Once I find the taxi rank and give the address to the driver, the nerves start worming their way back inside my chest. I don't even try to stop myself from biting my thumbnail as we drive through the picturesque town, my knee jangling against the empty front passenger seat. I'm mere minutes away from meeting these men who are adored by hundreds of thousands of people all across the globe.

How can I possibly compare with that?

You don't, I tell myself gently. *Take the pressure off. You're just here for them to play with. No one's going to care about you. The audience watches for Daddy and his men.*

I can be small and good. I know I can. That's all I focus on as the taxi makes its way down a winding lane leading up to a solitary cottage. For a second, my fears and worries vanish as I gasp, hardly believing I'm going to be staying in such a stunning place. It has a thatched roof and the signature Tudor style of white stone walls and black wooden beams. As autumn has begun, there aren't really any flowers in the garden, but it's immaculately kept. Wisteria frames all around the front door, and in summer, I bet it's a riot of purple blossoms.

Bloody hell. There's even a stream running by the property with a wooden arched footbridge crossing over it. I immediately want to Instagram everything to all forty-seven of my followers, but that was also part of the NDA. No social media posts about this until Daddy and Honipot have posted their content.

The taxi stops in front of the wooden gate, and I pay the driver with trembling fingers, telling him to keep the change. I only have my backpack with me as Mr. Cundall said I didn't need any fancy clothes, which is lucky because I don't have anything like that. I shrug the bag over my shoulders and watch the car make a remarkable three-point turn in such a narrow dirt road, then wait until it's completely out of sight.

I want this moment to be special. Private. That might seem silly, considering that I've agreed to be filmed in the most intimate way possible for thousands upon thousands of people to see. But right now, I just want this memory to be all mine so I can cherish it.

Yes, I am terrified. But I am also saving myself and my mum from financial ruin, not to mention that this is the bravest, craziest thing I've ever done.

I take a deep breath, unlatch the gate, then make my way down the garden path.

Before I can knock, the door opens.

And then there they are.

GOLDEN

Daddy is just as big and strong-looking as he is in the videos. He's only wearing a pair of grey jogging bottoms, and I try not to let my gaze flick to the outline of his huge cock resting on his thigh. It's impossible to ignore the expanse of hairy chest he has on display, but after a second or two, I manage to tear my gaze up to meet his dark, stormy eyes.

I don't exactly gulp, but I certainly swallow hard. He's a foot taller than me and twice the size, his demeanour menacing, like I've already displeased him. I bite my lip and try not to tremble under his stern gaze, but his mouth is downturned, and he crosses his arms as he takes me in.

I knew it. He's disappointed.

Desperate for something else to distract me, my eyes flick to the two figures flanking Daddy. I realise with a jolt that Papa is holding up a phone and there are lights in the shape of rings casting a soft glow on me. *He's already filming?* I don't feel prepared, but there's no backing down now.

Papa isn't nearly as bulky as Daddy, but he's still masculine under his polo shirt and chinos, classically handsome with soft brown hair, a square jaw, and warm hazel eyes. Dark hair creeps out from the neck of his shirt, hinting at the thick fur I know is underneath. His gaze is on his phone, presumably watching the footage he's recording, but he smiles, and I can't help but feel it's meant for me.

On Daddy's other side is Baby, jiggling from one foot to the other. I'd say Daddy is a bear and Papa is more of an otter. Baby is a proper bear cub, though, slightly chubby with his tummy poking out from a too-small T-shirt that has eighties Care Bears on it. Despite his young nature, his hair is already receding, so he keeps it closely shaven. I'm seized by the urge to run my hand over the fuzz. I wonder if he'll let me.

His cut-off denim shorts only just cover the curve of his juicy bum that I've seen both Daddy and Papa fucking

23

countless times. But right now, I don't see a porn star. I just see an excitable man a little older than me who is waving eagerly, like he's delighted I'm here.

"Well, boy," Daddy growls, making me jump as I jerk my attention back to him. "Are you going to come in?"

Dread rinses through me. I've already upset him. Oh *no, no, no!* I try and blink the tears back from my eyes.

"S-sorry, Daddy," I whisper, clutching onto my backpack straps and dropping my gaze. Maybe he won't want me after all, and he's going to send me back to the station I only just arrived from.

A thick finger and thumb suddenly touch my chin. It's the same move Mr. Cundall did to me in his office, but as Daddy tilts my chin up and I look into his dark brown eyes, the feeling is completely different.

Instead of revulsion, warmth and calmness wash through me. Daddy quirks his head, his expression still fierce, but his movement is gentle as he leans down...

And presses his hot, plump lips to mine, the scruff of his short beard scratching my skin.

I melt.

Everything is going to be okay now.

5

DADDY

THE GOLDEN ANGEL MELTS AGAINST ME LIKE BUTTER. So beautifully submissive and compliant. I felt his tension evaporate as soon as I took charge and made him kiss me. It's not always obvious from just a photo how someone is going to react in real life to being dominated. But from his sweet wide eyes and hopeful smile in the selfie, I sensed an honest, open need to be taken care of.

I'm glad not to be disappointed.

He moans into my mouth, and I chuckle. He probably has no idea what those filthy sounds from his pretty mouth do to me. I rub my already half-hard cock against his hip, so he's left with no doubt.

He gasps, and I use the opportunity to nip at his lower lip. "Welcome to our home, Goldie," I growl.

He blinks at me, looking a little drunk from the kiss. *Oh, sweet boy. If you think that was something, wait until I get my cock inside you.*

"Goldie?" he repeats.

I nod. "That's your name for this visit," I inform him. I

didn't even bother looking at the name on the file. He's my golden angel, and that's all that matters now.

His face splits into that gorgeous smile from the picture my men and I have been obsessing over the past few days. "Goldie," he agrees, his eyes shining up at me.

I rub one of those pretty curls between my fingers and thumb, feeling how silky it is. He really is a cherub.

I turn and gently take Papa's phone from him so I can continue filming. "Say hello to our guest, boys," I tell him and Baby.

Of course Baby eagerly bounds up to Goldie and throws his arms around him, nuzzling against his neck and rubbing his back. "We're so happy to have you here!" he cries. He cups his hands on either side of Goldie's startled face, brushing his thumbs over Goldie's high, rosy cheekbones. "Daddy's going to take such good care of you. We all are."

My mouth twitches into a glimmer of a smile. Baby's enthusiasm cracks through even my surly demeanour. It's one of the reasons I adore him so much. Everyone is welcome and included when Baby is around.

I run my hand down his back. "I think our pretty boy deserves a kiss. Don't you, Baby?"

He beams at me and bats his eyelashes. "Yes, Daddy." He turns back to Goldie, whose eyelids flutter closed as he leans in obediently to be kissed. I grunt appreciatively as I watch them, enjoying my two pretty boys getting to know one another. Oh, yes. I think they're going to be beautiful together.

I'm not the only one hungrily taking in the display. Papa closes the front door quietly behind Goldie, careful not to disturb or distract them. I nod to him, letting him know I want him to join in whilst I step back and capture it all on film.

Papa's answering smile is bashful and sweet, but the way

he slides his hands over the backs of both the boys' necks is commanding and delicious. Goldie and Baby shiver, breaking apart.

Papa presses a kiss to the corner of his husband's mouth, then turns to lock eyes with our new guest. "Hello, Goldie," he says, his voice warm and rumbly. I see the way Baby responds to it, even after all these years. "I'll be your Papa for the weekend. It's a pleasure to meet you."

"It's lovely to meet you, too, Papa," says Goldie, looking up at him through his eyelashes.

"May I kiss you as well?" Papa asks, running his thumb over the lower of Goldie's swollen lips.

Goldie nods, then seems to find his voice. "Y-yes, Papa. I'd like that very much."

"Good boy. Sweet boy," Papa says, and Goldie whimpers at the praise. "You are astonishingly beautiful. Thank you so much for coming to play with us this weekend."

"Thank you so much for inviting me," Goldie says breathlessly. "I still can't believe it, and I don't really know why. I mean, uh…"

I chuckle at his childlike manners, and Papa smiles, too. "You're a special boy," he tells Goldie, caressing the back of his neck possessively. "Of course we had to invite you to our home. You're going to be good for us, aren't you?"

"So good," Goldie agrees with an eager nod, his words still nervous and fluttery.

It's been a long time since I played with someone like this. Well, I don't think I've ever played with anyone quite like Goldie. But I haven't had the pleasure of dominating someone so pure and in desperate need of validation.

Baby is a naughty boy who can sometimes get bratty when he wants a good spanking. Papa is good and sweet for me, but he doesn't need reassurance like Goldie seems to. It's as if he craves it like oxygen. I suspect he hasn't had anyone caring for him or telling him how wonderful he is much in his life.

Well, now he has us. If only for a little while.

Papa kisses Goldie hard, hugging both boys to him in his strong arms. Baby bites his lip and runs his hand up and down Goldie's flank. I like what I'm seeing. Three gorgeous men, all mine to command and take care of, all pleasuring each other.

I hold the phone with one hand, getting in a bit closer to get a good shot of the kiss, then drop my other hand to palm my thickening erection through my joggers.

Yes, it's time to take this welcome party up a notch.

"Goldie, come here," I instruct. Papa breaks off the kiss to release him, and I hand the phone over to him. Goldie moves in front of me, his mouth bright pink and his pupils blown. "Good boy," I say because it's true, but also because I want to hear his breath hitch.

He doesn't let me down.

"So good," I murmur.

He stands still as I push the straps of his bag over his shoulders and take the rucksack off him. Baby scampers forward, eager to take it, and hugs it to his chest. He's being extra obliging this evening. I can tell how much he wants our newcomer to feel welcome.

I agree.

I take Goldie's hand and place it against my cock, hard and pulsing through the cotton trousers. Goldie's eyes go wide with shock, and he gasps. I smirk.

"See how happy you've already made Daddy?"

"Y-yes, Daddy," he stammers. He looks between me and my award-winning cock like he's dealing with a skittish horse that might bolt on him.

Well, like a horse, I've certainly got something for him to ride.

I lean in to murmur in his ear as my hand slips over his arse, caressing it. "Were you a good boy for Daddy? Are you all ready for his big cock?"

He splutters adorably, like a blushing virgin. "Y-yes, Daddy. I'm wearing the, um, *plug.*"

I grin at his embarrassment. I wonder if he's ever worn one before, then decide from the way he's going crimson that he almost certainly hasn't.

"Good boy, obeying your Daddy and trying new things. I'm proud of you."

He moans as his eyes flutter closed. I press harder, finding the base of the butt plug through his jeans and stimulating it. He gasps and whimpers, bringing his small hands up to support himself against my chest. His warm palms against my skin feel good.

I need more.

I kiss his lips again, then drag the bottom one through my teeth. "Such a pretty mouth," I growl, rubbing the lower lip hard with the pad of my thumb. "I think it would look delicious wrapped around my monster cock. Why don't you be a good boy and drop to your knees for Daddy?"

He freezes.

I blink, not sure what's going on.

"D-Daddy?" he whispers. It almost sounds like a plea. For a second, I think he's going to safe word.

Over a blow job.

What's going on here?

"Yes, sweet boy?" I tilt his chin to make him look at me.

There are tears in his eyes, and he's trembling. Is this an act? Because as far as I'm concerned, good, sweet boys should only beg and tremble and cry because I'm fucking them so hard that they're desperate to come.

He closes his eyes and takes a deep breath. "I might...I might not be very good at that," he says so quietly I barely

HELEN JULIET

catch it. "Actually, I don't think I am. Good at it, I mean. I'm sorry. I don't want to let you down."

This has got to be an act. An aspiring porn star who doesn't think he's good at giving head? It's hard to fuck that up, really. A hot, needy mouth on my dick is always going to be a good time. I even like a little teeth, so he couldn't even get that wrong.

"You won't let Daddy down if you do as he says," I assure him. "Because you're a good, sweet boy who's eager to make Daddy happy, isn't that right?"

His eyes finally flutter back open. "Oh, yes, Daddy. Yes, I want to make you happy."

"You don't need to worry now that you're here. Daddy's just going to tell you what to do, all right?"

He nods, and I rub the side of his neck. "What's your colour, sweet boy?"

He swallows, seeming to really think about it. "Green, Daddy."

I hum appreciatively. "Sweet like honey," I say, running my fingers through those golden locks and giving them a sharp tug. He gasps and bites his lip, then grinds his cock through his jeans against my thigh.

There we go. Much better. I decide it has to be an act, and I'm into it so long as he listens to me when I tell him he's good and perfect. I don't like my boys disagreeing with me when I'm the one who knows best.

"Now, I believe I asked you to get down and suck Daddy's big, fat dick, didn't I, Goldie? Papa and Baby want to see how greedy you are for my cock."

Goldie blinks and glances at my men like he'd forgotten they were there. He blushes adorably, but from the way his breathing gets heavier, I know he's already getting off on the idea of being watched.

I think our sweet golden angel is pretty innocent for

someone who's decided to get into adult entertainment. But in my eyes, that only makes him more scrumptious. He's *mine*, and I'm going to show him so many new, exciting things.

I'm going to *ruin* him for other men.

6

GOLDIE

My nerves leap back into my chest as Daddy places a huge hand on my shoulder and pushes me to my knees. Robert always complained I was terrible at giving head, but then he'd always insist I do it anyway, holding my head so I couldn't pull away.

Then he'd laugh at me as I tried my best to pleasure him.

I want to be good for Daddy *so* badly, and I want to impress Papa and Baby who are watching us. The camera is almost irrelevant. I don't care about a faceless audience. These men have all been so nice to me, making me feel special and welcome. I don't want to let them down.

Daddy caresses my hair then cups the side of my face. "Take Daddy's cock out and suck it, golden angel. I'm tired of waiting."

My breath catches. "I'm sorry, Daddy," I whisper.

He shakes his head. "I know you're a good boy. Are you scared it's too big?"

I nod because that seems better than thinking about horrible Robert, and it's actually true as well. I can see through the loose jogging bottoms that Daddy is already pretty hard, and I'm kind of worried if I'll be able to get my mouth around his girth. Also, I feel like being concerned that his cock is too big is actually a nice compliment.

Sure enough, Daddy grins, and my heart warms.

"You can do it, sweet boy," he says. He rubs his thumb over my lower lip, then pushes it into my mouth. I suck obediently, and his mouth drops into an O-shape. "Fuck. Pretty. Isn't he pretty, boys?"

I glance out of the corner of my eye to see Baby standing in front of Papa. They're both watching us whilst Papa gropes Baby's cock through his undone shorts and kisses his neck. The camera is perched on a nearby table, filming us all.

Baby nods and pants. "So pretty, Goldie. You can do it. Daddy's cock tastes yummy, and it'll make your jaw ache in the best way."

I take a deep breath through my nose, still sucking Daddy's thumb, and relax. Daddy is in charge. He'll tell me if I'm rubbish at it. I know he will. All that matters is that I'm good by trying my best.

I feel kind of floaty, like my body isn't quite mine, as I pop off Daddy's thumb and reach up to pull the waistband of his joggers down. He doesn't move at all as I slide them over his hips and down his thick, hairy thighs, allowing his giant cock to spring free.

I gulp, eyeing it like an opponent. I know I'm pretty small and skinny, but I swear it's about the size of my forearm and fist.

How am I going to get that up my *arse,* let alone in my mouth?

Daddy cards his fingers through my hair, and I hear the slapping sound of Papa jerking Baby off. They're getting hot watching *me.* I'm already turning them on. I just need to hold on to this floaty feeling of not worrying and simply doing as I'm told. I'll be a good, obedient boy for Daddy and make him happy. I'll make them all happy, and then they won't regret choosing to invite me here.

Warm pride at the thought spurs me on as I reach with my hand to wrap my fingers around the base of Daddy's cock, then lick the leaking, uncut tip like a lollypop.

"That's it, golden angel," Daddy groans. His nails scrape over my scalp, making me shudder. "Take it all. Let Daddy fuck your pretty face."

I stretch my lips around the head, pushing it against my cheek as I try and remember everything I've read about giving good head. I did a lot of research after Robert's complaints, but nothing is quite the same as practising on a real cock.

I rub my tongue against the shaft and stroke the root with my hand, twisting and squeezing. It's like steel sheathed in velvet and tastes salty and musky, like pure, undistilled man. Much better than Robert's cheesy knob, which I will never, ever think of again after this heavenly experience.

"Yes, sweet boy, *yes*," Daddy hisses.

He tightens his grip on my hair, rocking my head faster over his length. I blink tears from my eyes, determined not to splutter as I strive to deep throat this monster as much as I can.

"So good for your Daddy, so perfect. Your Papa and Baby think you're a good, needy little boy, don't they?"

"So fucking hot," Baby rasps, his words ragged as Papa teases him.

"You're stunning, Goldie," says Papa warmly. "So good for our Daddy. Just like he knew you would be."

I blink back tears again, but these aren't from gagging.

I only walked through the door twenty minutes ago. How is this dream real? I've wanked off countless times to the videos these impossibly hot men have made. I feel like I've known them for years. How am I here now, getting this praise with such an enormous cock tickling my tonsils? It's so surreal. It helps me float away even more.

I don't have to make any decisions. I'm not responsible for anything. Daddy will tell me how to be good for him, and I'll do it. It's that simple.

He drops his head back and grunts like an animal. Then he suddenly lets go of my hair to grab my arm and haul me back up to my feet. Saliva dribbles down my chin, but before I can wipe it off, he's kissing me brutally.

"You're a naughty boy for lying to your Daddy," he growls when he finally releases my mouth. My heart drops. How was I *naughty*? But it turns out it's not a bad kind of naughty, not really. He tuts and raises an eyebrow. "You told your Daddy you were bad at sucking cock. I'm going to make you suck Papa's and Baby's cocks now, so you can see how wrong you were."

I'm shaking from adrenaline. He's going to *make* me suck them off. I don't have a choice, and I love it more than I can even say.

"Yes, Daddy. I'm s-sorry, Daddy," I splutter. "I won't lie again."

Fuck Robert. Daddy says I'm a cock-sucking *champion*.

Daddy swats my arse, making me jump. "Over there, now. Crawl for Daddy. Take turns making my men happy. They're hungry for your greedy little mouth."

As I drop down on all fours, Daddy kicks his joggers off, leaving him gloriously naked. His muscles aren't sharp or particularly defined as they're hidden under a cuddly layer of fat and all that thick, fuzzy hair. I imagine him pinning me down with his whole, formidable body and get even harder in my jeans than I am already.

Papa is still standing behind Baby. He releases his cock and wraps his hand around Baby's throat, and they both watch me as I kneel in front of them. Baby's cock is kind of short and chubby like the rest of him, and it's standing to attention after the way Papa has been playing with it. Before I even taste it, I decide I love it. It's cute and sweet, just like him.

I easily get it all in my mouth, and I suck and lick it for my life. Baby thrusts into me, grunting and gasping.

"Is that nice, Baby?" Papa asks.

I look up at them through my eyelashes, my tummy fluttering in anticipation. I want my new friend to like it, to like *me*.

Baby nods, Papa's hand still around his throat. "So good, Papa. You're going to love his hot, pretty mouth."

I feel like I've been bathed in sunshine.

"I'm sure I will, Baby," Papa murmurs. "Say thank you to Daddy for getting us such a lovely toy to play with. Doesn't Daddy take such good care of us?"

"T-thank you, Daddy," Baby gasps. He looks behind me, then down into my eyes. "I love our pretty golden angel. I want to keep him."

Keep me?

I drop my eyes, unable to cope with the feelings swelling in my chest. It's only a scene. He's just saying that as part of the performance. This is only for the weekend.

Still, I can't deny that was *really* nice to hear.

I open my eyes again as I feel Daddy's hand back in my hair. He leans in to kiss Baby, who reaches for his big, hard cock unprompted.

"You're so welcome, Baby," Daddy rumbles against his mouth. "He's all ours for the whole weekend to do whatever we want to him. He's going to be our good, needy little boy."

I moan. I'm *theirs*. I belong to *them*.

Even if it's only for a little while, I'll take it. For once in my life, I'm not responsible for anything. I don't have to worry or feel like I have the weight of the world on my shoulders. All I have to do is just like Mr. Cundall said.

Lie back and think of England, whilst Daddy, Papa, and Baby do whatever beautiful, dirty things they want to me.

I'm in heaven.

7

PAPA

I GROAN AND LET MY HEAD THUD BACK AGAINST THE WALL, watching Goldie swallow my cock like a boss. As turned on as I am, my heart also aches. He looked positively stricken when Daddy first instructed him to suck his dick, claiming in a trembling whisper that he was no good, clearly distraught at the idea of disappointing Daddy.

Who broke him down like that? Who made him think his pretty mouth was anything less than perfect?

Whoever they are, they're obviously a raving lunatic. I've had my cock sucked by countless men, and this sweet boy is a natural. His technique isn't complicated, but it's earnest and enthusiastic. He's making me feel like taking me into his mouth is the greatest gift I could bestow on him.

Daddy and Baby are pressed to my sides. Daddy is naked and has his hand under my polo shirt, pinching and rubbing my nipples as he watches Goldie slurp and suck my cock. Baby is mostly still dressed, just with his cute cock protruding from his open shorts. He's cuddled up to my other side, my phone back in hand so he can get a point-of-view shot of Goldie's flawless performance.

Goldie looks up at me, saliva running down his chin, batting his wet, spiky lashes. I reach down and brush a stray tear from his cheek from where he's been gagging, and he leans into my touch. Moaning.

"So good, angel," I tell him.

It's been so long since I've had a boy who needed to hear my affirmations so badly. Baby used to be like that, and I couldn't be prouder of the gorgeous, sometimes bratty boy he's grown into. But there's something really special about knowing that a sub *needs* you in that way. Like his life depends on your good opinion.

It's so easy to give it to someone like Goldie, who's beautifully compliant and eager to please. It's like working with warm putty. I have no doubt that this weekend Daddy— with my and Baby's help—will create a masterpiece.

The calmness in his wet eyes is breath-taking. He's gone from trembling with fear to trembling with pleasure. I love the powerful feeling that gives me. Our Daddy did that. I'm helping him now. I want to wrap him up in a hundred blankets and whisper to him how perfect he is.

Maybe whilst stroking his cock. I bet he has a pretty one.

I love the different sizes all three of us have and how much we each adore and worship the others'. Baby was shy about his size before we met, but it didn't take me much time at all to make him understand how gorgeous it is. I'm smaller than Daddy's monster that Baby and I both love to ride, but that makes me perfect for warming up tight, hot holes for Daddy to then squeeze into.

I hope he'll let me fuck Goldie first, even though he's been wearing the butt plug. I want to feel his most intimate area envelop me. I want to let the world see me be the first one to fuck that tight hole and make him scream in the best way.

"Stop, Goldie," Daddy commands.

I groan and nestle my head against Daddy's furry pec in

discomfort as Goldie immediately obeys, popping off my cock and sitting down on his heels. He looks up at us as his chest rises and falls, waiting for his next instruction like an obedient little puppy.

"Good boy," Daddy tells him, and Goldie's eyes blaze with pride. "Stand up now, and let us look at you. Ah—*no,*" he snaps as Goldie goes to wipe his chin. "Daddy wants to see the evidence of all the fun you've been having. You loved sucking Daddy's cock and his men's cocks, didn't you? You were greedy for them all."

"Yes, Daddy," Goldie says, wobbling slightly as he gets to his feet. He's breathless with blown pupils and a sizeable bulge in his jeans.

Daddy rubs my tummy, and I moan, nuzzling his chest more and inhaling the scent of his arousal.

"I think you're all wearing far too many clothes for Daddy's liking. Golden angel, strip for us. Let your lovers see how pretty you are."

Goldie bites his lip, and I see that flicker of fear return. I glance up at Daddy, who scowls. He doesn't like to be disobeyed, because he knows what's best for all of us. But Goldie is definitely shy, and I don't want him to feel he has to safe word out of his very first scene with us.

"What's the matter, Goldie?" I ask gently. "Don't you know how beautiful you are?"

"*So* beautiful," Baby adds, palming his own cock.

I smile at how much my gorgeous husband wants to play with our new toy. Usually, our guests are big gym bunny types who don't think twice about topping Baby. I know he always loves that just fine, but I can see his excitement at having another bottom to play with. It's a different kind of energy, and I think we're all loving the change of pace.

So long as Goldie is happy, too.

"Daddy's right, sweet boy," I say. "We want to see all of you. Don't keep him waiting."

"I…I'm so skinny, though," Goldie whispers, glancing at the camera nervously. "Sorry, I shouldn't say things like that, should I? Are we live?"

I blink in confusion. Doesn't he know how this works? If he's getting into the industry, surely he should have researched that?

That's something we can talk about later. The only thing that matters now is reassuring our golden angel.

"No, sweet boy," I say kindly. "I'll edit all this out. And it's important you ask questions if you're uncomfortable. Isn't it, Daddy?"

Daddy is frowning, though. "It's important that good boys listen to their Daddies," he growls. "Daddy said you were beautiful, golden boy, and now he wants to see all of you. Would your Daddy lie to you?"

Goldie visibly sags, a smile creeping onto his face as he looks reverently at Daddy. "No, of course not," he says. "I'm sorry for not believing you, Daddy. I'll be good for you now."

"That's it, precious boy," Daddy purrs as Goldie whips his thin, silver-and-grey-striped jumper over his head. He drops it to the floor, leaving his golden hair in a staticky halo around his head.

I'd say he was slim rather than skinny, with pebbled pink nipples and just a hint of blond fuzz trailing down from his navel and disappearing below his jeans. He's blushing as he pulls off his trainers and socks, but he doesn't hesitate as he unbuttons his jeans. With one last fortifying breath, he shoves them down along with his underwear, kicking the last of his clothes away.

He's quivering as he drops his hands to his sides, but then he manages to look up at us, the wild look in his eyes clearly seeking our approval.

"Fucking gorgeous," Daddy growls, speaking for us all. "Touch your cock for us, golden angel. Let us see you."

Goldie licks his lips, his gaze not wavering from Daddy's as he lifts his hand and wraps it around his cock. Despite his slim frame and medium height, I'd say his dick is about the same size as mine, although his curves slightly to the left. My mouth waters to taste it as he slowly strokes himself off.

"So good for your Daddy, sweet boy," Daddy says. "Come here now. Don't let yourself go."

Goldie is panting as he moves closer to us, still touching himself deliciously. Daddy grabs his chin and plunders his mouth with his tongue. His lips are positively bruised from all our kissing so far, and I know we're nowhere near done with him yet.

"Undress my men for me, Goldie," Daddy murmurs against his lips before taking the camera off Baby. "I need all my boys naked and gagging for my big cock. Can you do that for me?"

"Y-yes, Daddy," he replies reverently, then turns to me, his eyes shining in anticipation.

I love being undressed by someone else. Usually, this isn't something we do with our playdates. When we're alone, Daddy loves ripping my clothes off, or sometimes he'll tell Baby to do it, just like he's done with Goldie now. It feels more intimate than when he had his lips wrapped around my cock, and I nuzzle my nose against his as his fingers brush my stomach, preparing to lift my polo shirt up.

"Good boy. Pretty boy," I remind him. I'm rewarded with a hum and a shy smile before he eases off my shirt and drops it to the floor. My fly is already undone from the blowjob, so he tugs my chinos down and yanks off my socks to finish the job. As he stands, I pull him in for a kiss. "Thank you," I murmur against his mouth.

"You're welcome, Papa," he says sweetly, running his hands over the hair on my chest.

That just leaves Baby in his clothes. The two boys giggle as Goldie peels off the Care Bear T-shirt, then shucks down the booty shorts. Baby grabs Goldie's face for a messy kiss, and Goldie rests his hands on Baby's soft tummy.

They look totally adorable together.

Daddy passes the camera back to me then holds out his hand to the pretty boys. "Goldie, come to your Daddy now."

Goldie smiles at Baby and gives him one last kiss on the nose before obeying the command and taking Daddy's hand. Daddy kisses him hard again, first stroking Goldie's cock, smearing pre-cum down the length, then reaching around to rub the end of the butt plug.

"I think it's time we took this out and filled you up with something hot and wet, don't you, golden angel?"

Goldie blinks, already sex drunk. "Yes, please, Daddy," he moans.

Daddy leads him by the hand down the corridor. "Then Daddy says it's bedtime. But no one is allowed to sleep yet."

He winks over his shoulder at Baby and me, and my heart soars. After all the scenes we've done over the years, I can tell when something is going to be special.

I have a feeling this is going to be *sensational.*

Baby pats my arm, and for a moment I pause filming. We can pick back up in the bedroom in a minute, and right now, I want to give my husband my full attention.

"Yes, Baby?" I say, smiling as I kiss along his jaw.

"Papa," he moans. *"Papa."*

"I'm right here, Baby. What is it?" He licks his lips and searches my face, almost like he's nervous. "Baby?" I prompt, suddenly worried.

"I really like him," he blurts out, and my worries vanish as quickly as they'd arrived. "I know we just met him, but he's special...don't you think?"

I run my hand over Baby's close-cropped hair, the prickling sensation making me shiver. Then I take both our cocks in hand, squeezing them together. "I think he's a treasure," I say truthfully. "But I especially love how much you're lighting up around him. I think you two are going to be beautiful to watch playing together."

He nods eagerly, his grey eyes sparkling. "We're going to make you and Daddy so fucking hot, Papa," he says breathlessly. "I'll be naughty, and Goldie will be nice."

I swat his luscious arse, making it wobble. "And it's not even Christmas yet," I comment as he giggles. "Come on, then. We better not keep Daddy waiting."

I ponder Baby's words as I lead him down to the bedroom. There's something new about our dynamic as a foursome that I have to admit is warming my heart. I know we've booked Goldie to play for the weekend, but I'm already finding myself wondering if he might stay for longer or agree to come back another time. I like what he's doing to all three of us.

Is it too soon to be thinking about the future?

8

GOLDIE

THIS IS TOO MUCH AND YET NOT ENOUGH. MY MIND IS PURE white noise as I float above myself, my body awash with too much sensation to truly process everything. I love it, mostly because since my thoughts are quiet, all that's left is the tortuous pleasure consuming me.

I'm in Daddy's bedroom that he shares with Papa and Baby. I've seen countless videos of this space, and now here I am with them on the ridiculously enormous bed. When we first entered, Daddy picked me up and deposited me on the mattress, then proceeded to remove the plug and eat out my hole whilst Papa and Baby watched. Papa might have set up some more cameras. I'm honestly not sure.

My attention was on more immediate matters.

Then Daddy left me, naked, trembling, and panting as he strode off to sit in a plush armchair in the corner of the room. He'd just said, "You know what I want."

Before I could worry that I had no idea what that meant, Papa and Baby had crawled up on the bed with me, manhandling me onto all fours.

Then Baby had fed me his cock again whilst Papa lubed

up my arse and pushed his hot, hard cock deep inside me. The plug had helped with the stretching, but that bit of rubber was *nothing* compared to having a throbbing cock forced inside. I would have cried out if my mouth hadn't been full of Baby's chubby length.

"That's it, boys," Daddy growls. I can just see from the corner of my eye that he's stroking himself as he watches us, and my whole body *burns.* "Fuck our little golden angel good and hard. He loves it, don't you, angel?" I moan as loudly as I can with my mouth full, making Daddy chuckle darkly. *Bloody hell,* I love that sound. "Of course you love it. You're such a good, greedy boy, made to take our cocks all night long."

I quiver on my hands and knees as Papa's thrusts push my mouth over Baby's cock again and again. Baby strokes my face with one hand, his other resting on his tummy. Our eyes lock, and he beams down at me.

"So good, angel," he whispers like it's our little secret. "Your mouth feels amazing. I love it. And you're *so* pretty."

My eyes flutter closed at the praise, allowing it to wash over me. I feel fucking *gorgeous* under the red hot gazes of these three men.

I thought my presence here would be almost irrelevant to them. That they would make me feel like an accessory. But right now, I'm the *star*. It's as if I'm onstage in the spotlight. In real life, the idea of performing in front of people or public speaking would make me pass out from nerves. But with these three men, I'm lapping up the attention like I was born to shine for them.

Papa hits my prostate, and I wail, my breathing ragged through my nose. He's holding my arse open as his cock impales me again and again. He's just so *confident.* He knows what he wants—or what Daddy wants him to do, more accurately—and he's just taking it. I've never had sex like this. By removing any decisions for me, Daddy's made me feel confident, too. Like I can do anything.

More than that. I feel like for the first time in my life I'm actually *good* at sex.

My hard cock is leaking and bouncing against my belly as I get fucked from both ends. I can feel my climax building inside me, and I wonder if I might actually be able to come untouched. Daddy didn't say anything about me coming, though, and my gut instinct urges me to wait. Daddy knows best. He'll tell me when the time is right.

If Mr. Cundall had informed me that I'd be doing something so graphic within an hour of stepping through the front door, I probably would have bolted. This is so far out of my usual comfort zone I'm practically in outer space.

But that's the old me talking. The new me—Goldie—feels totally at home being used by two gorgeous men like a treasured plaything. Daddy keeps saying I was made to take all three of their cocks, and I'm starting to believe he's right.

How am I ever going to have regular, vanilla sex again?

I can worry about that later. Right now, all that matters is that I'm good for Daddy, and that means pleasing Papa and Baby.

Daddy knows what he wants, though. I need to remember that and stop worrying. He's in charge, and it's wonderful.

"Come for me, boys," he commands, still leisurely stroking himself. "Paint our golden angel and make him even prettier. I want him ready for me."

Immediately, both Papa and Baby pull their cocks out of me, and I look up to watch Baby masturbate furiously, his eyelids heavy and his gaze once again locked with mine. I can hear Papa jerking off as well, the tip of his cock bouncing against my bum.

When Baby drops his head back with a groan, I blink rapidly as he starts to come. I don't want to miss a second of such an erotic sight, but I don't want to spoil things by getting jizz in my eye either. Thick, white ropes streak along my face, neck, and chest, making me feel marked like an animal. Within seconds, there are also hot spurts along my thighs and back as well as down my crack. Papa's fingers smear his cum all over my hole, pushing some inside easily with his slippery fingers.

I'm a dripping, trembling mess, and I've never felt more beautiful in my life. I try and stay as still as I can despite my quivering limbs and deep, shaky breaths. I sense Daddy stand and move over to us, then whimper as he gently touches my chin to make me look at him.

"A work of art," he murmurs.

He grabs Baby's jaw and kisses him hard. Papa has moved up the bed beside me, and Daddy gives him an equally brutal kiss. Then they both flop down against the pillows on the left and right, and Daddy sits himself up between them, his legs resting on either side of my hands. His cock stands proudly in front of my face like a flagpole. Honestly, you could fly the Union Jack off that thing.

He crooks a finger at me. "Come give Daddy a kiss, sweet boy."

I take a breath to steady myself, then crawl up to meet him on shaking limbs. This kiss isn't as aggressive, and he licks away the cum that splattered on my lips.

"Are you having fun, angel?"

I nod frantically. "I love it, Daddy," I say breathlessly. "Thank you so much. Papa and Baby made me feel so good."

"You made them feel good, too," Daddy says with a feral grin, running his finger down some of the cum streaked across my chest. "I knew you would. Now it's time to make Daddy feel good."

He spanks my arse hard, and I gasp as the delicious pain zings through me. The adrenaline wakes me up and clears my head slightly. I'm still exhausted, but my heart is racing again.

"How, Daddy?" I beg. "I'll do anything you want. I'm your good boy."

I almost can't believe these words are tumbling from my mouth. Robert always told me to shut up and stop babbling because it ruined his buzz, but Daddy's eyes smoulder at my dirty talk. I'm almost angry that I put up with such terrible sex from my ex. No wonder the porno he tried to make failed so miserably. That, and the *accusations,* which I can well believe.

"You are my good boy," Daddy murmurs, pushing his thumb into my mouth again for me to suck. "Daddy is going to lie back and relax whilst you do all the work. Ride his monster cock like a stallion."

Despite all my best efforts, the fear comes back. *I'm* the one who's supposed to lie back and think of England. Now he wants me to do all the work to please him? What if I do it wrong?

I've hesitated too long, I know. Daddy's eyes go dark. "Are you being naughty, little angel?" he growls.

"I-I don't want to be bad," I whisper. "I don't want to get it wrong and make you unhappy. I don't think I'll be good at it."

Without warning, Daddy seizes my hips, lifts me up, and *shoves* my arse onto his throbbing erection. I gasp. Despite the plug and Papa's gorgeous cock, it's still so big it burns.

But then something magical happens, and bliss washes through me.

The burning is all I have to focus on, the pain distracting me from any other noisy thoughts. And because Daddy manhandled me, I know I'm where he wants me.

"Oh, Daddy," I gasp, rocking myself so I ease down his hard member. "It's so big. I don't think it'll fit!" I liked the way my worrying about his cock size made him hot before, and sure enough, his eyes blaze again.

"You're going to take all of Daddy's cock because you're a good little angel, aren't you? You don't want to disappoint Daddy, do you?"

Absolutely not. I shake my head and dig my fingers into his hairy chest as I use his words to spur me on, taking him in deeper.

"I love it, Daddy. It feels so good!" I squeak.

I'm so full it's like his cock has reached up through me and is choking me inside my throat. I focus on the perfect pain, the overwhelming discomfort. I also allow myself to notice the sweat dripping down my body, the trickling sensation tracing patterns along my skin. My neglected cock feels like it wants to explode.

"Daddy," I whine. "Daddy, *please."*

Daddy's hungry look just makes me harder for him as I bounce on his huge length. He shifts leisurely beneath me, keeping his promise and not thrusting up at all, making me do the work. He rubs my lips and makes me suck his thumb once more. Papa and Baby are watching us intently, Papa with his phone back in hand again, filming me closely.

I'm not sure how much longer I can keep this up. But I *must.* Daddy *needs* me to.

I lean farther down, ignoring the way my thighs are burning as I begin to really piston myself. I want to make my Daddy come so badly. I want to be good more than anything. I can do this. *I can do this.*

Finally, that composure slips a little from Daddy's face. He drops his head back and grunts, his hands moving over my hips. He still doesn't thrust against me, but his hands help me speed up. All the while, he never takes his intense gaze off me. His eyes may be drooped, but his attention doesn't waver from me.

"That's it, golden angel," he rasps. "Keep going. You're being just perfect for your Daddy."

"Yes, Daddy, yes," I whimper, unable to be any more articulate than that.

Just as I feel Daddy's hips start to twitch, finally meeting my thrusts, he suddenly rolls us over. I gasp as he looms over me, my heart skipping a beat in fear. But this isn't like the other fears I've had tonight. I'm not worried that I won't be good enough.

I'm frightened that Daddy is so big and on top of me that he could do *anything* he wanted to me and I couldn't stop him. The realisation is so sublime I have to arch my back and gnash my teeth to stop myself from coming that very instant.

Daddy pulls roughly out of me, then straddles me. I moan at the loss, my hole spasming. "Be still, sweet boy," Daddy growls.

I landed with my hands above my head and my legs flopped between Daddy's tree trunk thighs. I breathe deeply, feeling myself go pliant like Daddy wants. A true pillow princess. Daddy's smile is triumphant, and he captures my mouth for a searing kiss.

"Good boy, sweet angel," he says as he begins to wank himself off furiously above me. "You look so pretty covered in cum. You're ours now. Our golden boy."

"Yours," I whisper, my throat tight. I know I'm borderline delirious, but I really do feel like theirs, like I actually belong to them. I know that it's not real, but in my floaty state I let myself pretend. Just for now.

Daddy throws his head back and roars, his cum gushing all over me like a fire hose. My breath hitches, and I have to close my eyes briefly as it sprays all over my face and heaving chest. It seems to go on forever, and eventually, I carefully blink my eyes back open to see him milking the last of his cum from his still-straining cock.

I did that. That mess was all for me.

Panting, Daddy leans back on his heels, looking down on me like he's surveying his work. Which I guess he is. He nods, obviously sending some unspoken signal, because then Papa and Baby are cuddled up to my sides, my arms still above my head. I feel exposed and vulnerable and tingly all over. I gasp and twitch as their lips kiss my neck and the sensitive skin under my arms. I didn't even know how nice it was to be kissed like that, and I squirm. Their fingers trace through all the goopy cum that's plastered all over my thighs, hips, and chest.

"You're fucking *gorgeous,*" Baby hisses excitedly into my ear. "Do you feel good, pretty angel?"

I'm so close to coming it brings tears to my eyes. But they're touching anything but my cock, and a sob escapes my chest as I nod frantically. "So good," I whisper back, turning to face him.

Baby kisses me sweetly. Then Papa grips my jaw to turn me to kiss him, too. "You're stunning, sweet boy," he murmurs, his words overflowing with sincerity. "So good for your Daddy."

"And good boys deserve rewards," Daddy says.

I turn again to see him pressed up along Baby's back, nibbling his ear. Then he reaches down and squeezes my throbbing cock. I can't help but cry out, but I manage not to close my eyes, keeping them locked on my Daddy.

"We're going to watch you come all over yourself now, golden angel," he says in a commanding tone. It's an order I'm desperate to comply with. He scoops up some of the slippery cum from my belly, using it to help his hand glide exquisitely along my length. "Come for your Daddy. You've been so very good."

I can't hold on any longer. I screw up my eyes and bellow from the bottom of my toes, my entire body shuddering as the orgasm rips through me. For a few seconds I can't catch my breath as I pulse cream all up myself, mingling it with all the cum from Daddy and Papa and Baby.

I'm a debauched mess. I'm a filthy, *naughty* boy.

And yet it feels *so good.*

9

DADDY

As soon as my golden angel comes his brains out, his eyes close and his breathing deepens. For a while, I just drink him in as he dozes, something warm curling in my chest, knowing that on some level he trusts us enough to do that. I appreciate we wore him out, but he wouldn't just sink into unconsciousness if there wasn't some part of him that believes he's safe and treasured.

I kiss Baby's neck, and he stirs. I don't think he was sleeping as well, rather just in deep contentment watching our new playmate.

"Did you like that, gorgeous?" I ask my sweet boy.

It's funny. Usually when we're working everyone is quite playful after the big finish, even if it's just the three of us, but especially when we have guests. However, there's a tranquillity in the air right now that warms my heart.

Baby sighs and looks up at me for a kiss, which I oblige him with. "That was *amazing*," he says softly, I guess not wanting to disturb our angel yet. "I loved it so much, Daddy. Thank you."

I rub his belly and nuzzle his nose. "Of course, my baby. I knew you'd like someone different for a change."

The truth is, I've been going through the motions for a while now, especially when it comes to Honipot. Cundall is the one who sends us playmates. It's been years since the three of us went cruising at a bar for fresh blood.

I think maybe I've been a neglectful Daddy, and the realisation curdles in my stomach. I bite my tongue, though, and refuse to let my anger show on my face. I *hate* letting my men down, but perhaps the meaningless hook-ups we've been filming haven't been as fulfilling as I'd supposed.

I meet eyes with Papa, wondering if his train of thought is similar to mine. I see the same overflowing satisfaction on his face as he watches his husband gently caress Goldie's damp hair. The room stinks deliciously of sex, but there's something else hanging in the air that's less tangible.

Promise, maybe?

All I know is that I'm glad Goldie is staying with us the whole weekend. I want to see how he is outside of a scene. Because right now he looks utterly magnificent covered in my cum and the cum of my men. He did exactly as he was told, and I didn't miss the blissed-out look on his face when I took charge and made him do precisely what I knew would make him feel best.

Maybe that's all he needs. A good time with us to show him what he's missing in his life. But there's a stubborn part of me that really doesn't like the idea of him going off and working with someone else any time soon. They might not understand what he needs. I can see him so easily getting hurt.

I don't know what that means exactly—do I want to book him with us exclusively? Train him to protect himself on other jobs?

Neither of those prospects sits quite right with me, and it pisses me off. It's not like me not to know what I want. *Fuck it.* I'm not thinking of anything beyond this weekend, this minute, from now on. That's something I *can* control.

I realise Papa's and Baby's fingers are entwined and resting on Goldie's chest as it rises and falls. I'm not what you'd call a sappy fuck, but that shit makes my heart swell, nonetheless. I haven't been paying attention and didn't notice that perhaps there was something missing in our relationship. But now I'm on high alert, and I can see that whatever is going on here is working very well. As if having Goldie be sent to us is reviving us, like a tonic or a balm.

"Papa," I murmur, meeting eyes with my very handsome man. "Will you take Baby to the shower and take care of him? He's been so good and deserves a nice reward."

Papa's eyes flick down to Goldie, the question clear in them. Usually when we have a playdate, I take care of Baby and let Papa sort out our guest if that's what the playdate wants. Papa thrives off aftercare, so I like to give him that opportunity. Often, though, our guests are fine to have a quick shower by themselves, then just require feeding before sleep. It's not really...tender. When it's just the three of us, I look after everyone.

But right now, I feel very strongly that my little angel needs me to help him before the four of us join together.

"It's okay," I assure Papa. "We'll follow you shortly. Then Daddy will make sure everyone is taken care of, all right?"

Papa smiles at me. I love how strong he is. He craves my domination, but in so many ways, he's my equal in this relationship. I don't know what I'd do without him.

He brings Baby's fingers to his lips, but Baby pouts. Papa has it in hand, though, so I just stroke Baby's tummy and gently kiss his neck, letting him know this isn't the end of anything. Just the beginning, actually.

"Let's go get nice and clean, my love," he tells our naughty boy, "so we can be ready to look after Goldie. He's had a long day."

"Oh!" says Baby, perking up right away.

I can't help but smile. Baby *always* wants to be doted on and doesn't have a toppy or Dom bone in his body. The fact he wants to help look after Goldie is an interesting development that I intend to nurture.

I press my lips to his shoulder. "Go on, now. Be good for Daddy. I promise to let you play with Goldie again soon."

"He needs a shower, too," Baby says, looking over his shoulder at me.

I arch an eyebrow. I like that he's anticipated my plan, but he should know better. I sort of love that he's being naughty for our new sweet boy, though.

"Are you telling Daddy how to do his job?" I growl.

Baby grins and curls his toes. "No, Daddy," he says cheekily.

I nip at his shoulder, making him gasp and flutter his eyes shut for a second. "Go. Shower. Be good for Papa," I instruct.

He nods and kisses my cheek. "Yes, Daddy," he says.

"Good boys," I say to both him and Papa as they manoeuvre themselves carefully off the bed and head towards the master bathroom. As their footsteps fade, I caress the side of Goldie's face. "Sweet angel," I say in a clear voice. "It's time to wake up now. I can't let you sleep yet."

"No, Daddy," he mumbles, his eyes screwing up as he rolls against me.

I bite my lip. Often our playmates are happy to call me 'Daddy' during a scene, but it's just an act. Goldie is pretty much asleep, so his subconscious actions speak volumes.

Is it wrong that I already feel like it's quite natural to be his Daddy after just a couple of hours? I remember the last

57

time I felt that urge so strongly, though, and sigh. This isn't the same as Papa and Baby. Lightning can't strike twice.

I'm going against my own rules. I'm only supposed to be thinking of the here and now, not beyond Monday morning. So I trace my thumb across Goldie's lower lip, kiss his cheek, then give his shoulder a little shake.

"You need to wake up now, sweet boy. You need a shower. Can you be good for your Daddy and open your eyes?"

I won't lie. It's a rush as he blinks sleepily and looks around until his eyes meet mine. I smile down at him and rub his chest. "Good boy. You've been so perfect tonight. Now will you let Daddy take care of you?"

He blinks a few more times before nodding. I help him sit up, then pull open the bedside drawer to my left where I'd stashed the bottle of sports drink earlier in anticipation of just this. Something about that adorable photo had hinted to me that our sweet angel wasn't used to being worn out and would need a little extra help with recovery.

It seems like since we ended the scene, the blue bruises under his eyes have become even more prominent, and I wonder what it is that's made my golden boy so exhausted out in the real world.

He lets me tip the drink carefully into his mouth, leaving his hands by his sides, trusting I'll do everything for him. He's right, of course, and pride glows from within me.

"Come on," I say when I'm satisfied that he's drunk enough. "Let's get you cleaned up." The cum is starting to dry and will be making him very uncomfortable, which I can't have.

I help him to his feet, but he stops and looks at the bed, touching the duvet with his small hand. "We need to change the sheets," he says.

He's right in that they're covered in cum, but that's *my* job, and not his concern. Still, the fact he even thought of it is another thing that makes him stand out from our usual playdates.

"It's fine, sweet boy," I say. I hold his hand and place my other one on his lower back, pulling him away. "You don't have to worry about anything like that. Daddy's here."

He melts into my side, and my breath hitches. He just feels so *right* cuddled up to me like that. I take little steps so he can keep up, steering him towards the bathroom.

It's all steamed up as we enter, and I'm glad to see Papa and Baby already under the double rainfall heads in the walk-in shower stall. They both have poufs covered in suds that they're lathering over each other's bodies. I squeeze Goldie's side.

"Look, angel. Our men are waiting for us. Shall we join them?"

He looks up at me in mild surprise, like he can't believe he's allowed to do that. I raise my eyebrows because I've said he can, so of course it's allowed, and I expect an answer.

"Yes, Daddy," he says shyly with a hopeful smile. "Yes, please."

As we step under the gloriously hot water, Papa and Baby move easily to encompass our angel, soaping him up and washing away all the mess we've spilt on him. His golden curls darken as they get wet, and I take charge of rubbing our shampoo and conditioner through it.

There. Now he smells like the rest of us, and something in my lizard brain is very happy with that.

You can't keep him forever, a nasty voice whispers in the back of my mind.

I tell it to fuck off. Realistically, I know Goldie has a whole life that I know nothing about and have no right to intrude on.

But as we dry him off and I lead him to our *actual* bedroom, the one where we sleep and never film in, I can't shut up the other voice that's getting much louder than the nasty one.

As I tuck my golden angel in and watch as he falls asleep again immediately, that voice is chanting *mine, mine, mine!*

And I can't say I particularly disagree with it.

10

GOLDIE

CONSCIOUSNESS COMES SLOWLY UPON ME. I BLINK MY EYES open and find myself in an unfamiliar bed.

I'm also not alone.

Memories from yesterday evening all come flooding back at once, and I quickly screw my eyes shut in case waking up somehow makes it all stop and go away.

That really happened.

For the past few days, I had been trying to wrap my head around the fact that I was really going to come and work with my favourite adult entertainers—some of the biggest stars Honipot has to offer. But the reality was so infinitely better than the expectation.

It's still early morning. By the kind of bright, watery light filtering around the drawn curtains, I'd say dawn has only recently broken. I realise this isn't the same bedroom that we played in last night—the one I know from their films. That one is fancy and grand, like a hotel room. But this one has tons of photos of the three of them in frames, trinkets from all over the world, lush green house plants, teddy bears, and film posters.

This is their *actual* bedroom. It has to be. I bite my lip and figure they must usually sleep with their playmates in here once the scene is done.

I should try and go back to sleep, but my mind is whirring, replaying everything that has happened since I stepped through the front door of this picturesque cottage.

But as usual when I'm left with my thoughts for too long, they start to twist into something bad. I recall how brazen I felt, like I was the star of the show, and then how all three of these amazing men had taken the time to wash *me* down in the shower.

Was I greedy? And not in a good way like Daddy had made it sound yesterday. Had I been selfish and taken liberties? I should have been much more attentive and made an effort to reciprocate their ministrations. After all, they're the ones doing *me* a favour and helping me clear my insurmountable debt.

Not that they know that. Now my worries morph into a sickening guilt.

Mr. Cundall said I couldn't tell them. He made it very clear that Robert's embarrassing fuck-up would sully the name of the whole production company, and no one else needed to know. But already my affection for these men is so deep I loathe the idea of lying to them. They think I'm trying to make my start in the porn industry when nothing could be further from the truth.

And then I feel a different kind of guilt and shame. I'm being silly, imaging that I'm already having feelings for these three. That's pathetic. *They* are in an established, loving relationship. *I'm* just a playmate for the weekend.

I feel a rustling in the enormous bed full of men and maybe hear some incredibly quiet murmuring, but I keep my eyes closed and pretend I'm asleep. This was such a bad idea. Maybe I'll call Mr. Cundall this morning and ask how much footage he'll need and whether or not last night will be enough. The thought of leaving today breaks my heart, but I'm being ridiculous. I don't want to lie to these men anymore, and I certainly don't want my childish, needy feelings to grow when they won't be reciprocated. In fact—

My thoughts shudder to a complete halt. I'd been so caught up in my own miserable worries that I hadn't been paying attention to how the weight in the bed was shifting.

And now I had a hot mouth wrapped around my cock.

My eyes fly open as I splutter and jerk my body. As I gasp for air I look frantically around, seeing Daddy and Papa grinning down at me. The duvet slips away, and Baby's cheeky face peeks out as he hungrily slurps down my cock.

"D-Daddy?" I stutter.

Somewhere in the back of my mind, I recall that part of the contract I signed was consent for the entire weekend to basically be jumped on whenever Daddy and his men want. That's why they have safe words—the classic green, yellow, and red—if I ever want to opt out. I'm shocked to be woken up like this, but as my senses come back to me, my heart starts to race, and I realise that I *love* it. Technically, I *do* have a choice in this. But feeling like I don't makes that delicious bliss come swooping back through me.

And they're not even *filming* unless there's a camera somewhere I can't see. Is this just for fun?

Daddy strokes my hair—which is undoubtedly a bird's nest—and kisses me gently. "Good morning, golden boy. Baby was worried you were having a bad dream, so we wanted something nice to wake you up. Do you like it?"

I nod frantically. This is the first time any of them have sucked me off, and Robert always insisted I did it for him, never wanting to reciprocate. But I fucking *love* having my dick sucked. Baby's hot mouth is swallowing me all the way to the back of his throat where my tip is rubbing, and I could almost come this very second.

But I take a shuddery breath and force myself to calm. I'm not going to ruin this by blowing my load right away.

"I love it, Daddy," I whimper. "Thank you, Baby, *thank* you."

I run my hand over his head, and it's just as wonderfully soft but slightly prickly as I'd imagined.

"Good boy," Daddy says. He bites my earlobe and pinches my nipple, making it hard and pebbly. I gasp and arch up, and he chuckles darkly. Lust pulses down through my cock, and Baby moans around it. "That's it, my sweet boys. Enjoy yourself. Take your time. You can come whenever you feel ready, golden boy."

I try and make it last, but Baby is too amazing. Before long he's jerking off my length and licking my tip as I start to spurt. I whimper and writhe through the orgasm, immediately going boneless.

I always want to pass out after sex—something else Robert called selfish. But Daddy laughs at me as Baby laps up the last of my cum like it's ambrosia.

"Sweet, sleepy boy," Daddy says fondly, caressing my neck and chest before cupping my jaw and kissing me. "But Daddy and his men aren't done with you yet. Wake up now. It's time to get to work."

I go to try and comply, but there's a spark in the back of my brain—the bit that's still vaguely functioning—that remembers how Daddy liked me protesting yesterday.

"No, Daddy," I whine, burying my face against his broad, hairy chest. "I'm *too* tired, and the bed is *too* full and *too* small."

A thrill flies through me as Daddy picks me up and hauls me onto my hands and knees. He grabs my chin, his eyes blazing as I blink away the sleep and manage to look into them.

As I'd hoped, the tiredness has evaporated.

"Are you being naughty?" Daddy growls. "Because naughty boys get punished."

"No, Daddy!" I squeak. "I'm sorry. I'll be good, I promise. I didn't mean to be bad! But Daddy and Papa and Baby have made me *so* sleepy. I don't know how to stay awake."

His grin is animalistic, and even though I've only just come, a jolt of lust shoots through me. "It's okay, golden angel. Daddy knows exactly how to keep you awake."

He nods at Papa and Baby, and even in my trembling, sex-dazed state, I marvel at the level of silent communication these men have together. Papa props himself up against the many pillows, Daddy settles next to him, and Baby crawls to flop on the other side. They're all naked with their erections standing tall and proud: little, huge, and just right. They stroke them, their eyes on me. I make a show of gulping like I'm nervous of them instead of absolutely gagging for all three.

"We've got a breakfast buffet for you, golden angel," Daddy purrs, his hand wrapped around his beastly member. "You're going to take turns sucking us all. If you're going to be a naughty, whiney brat, Daddy needs to give you something to fill that mouth with."

I lick my lips and nod, edging forward to reach for his ridiculous cock. "That's a much better idea, Daddy," I rasp. "I'm awake now, I promise. Thank you for making me be good again."

"Always, golden angel," Daddy says. He caresses the side of my face, then guides me down to swallow as much of his length as I can manage.

By making me do the things I secretly want to do anyway, Daddy forces almost all of the bad thoughts to float away.

The only one that lingers feels like a safety net, the voice trying to protect me from myself and my own foolish heart.

This isn't real. It's just pretend. It's only for a weekend. Don't catch feels.

But even that voice slips away as I move from cock to cock, my jaw aching and my eyes watering as I gag on each perfect one. When I'm not pleasuring them, the other two touch themselves and watch me. Sometimes they reach over and stroke my hair or rub my back. They tell me I'm pretty and perfect and such a good, greedy little boy.

I feel completely owned without a responsibility in the world beyond this bedroom.

I wish it would never end.

11

BABY

I'M SITTING IN THE SUN LOUNGE, WATCHING THE BIRDS dancing around the feeder down the bottom of the back garden. With the French doors open, there's a pleasant breeze drifting into the cottage, and I smile as I sip my mug of tea, enjoying my moment of peace.

It's only late morning, yet it feels like *so* much has happened since yesterday evening. I'm grateful for a brief respite alone to process my thoughts.

I love my life. Seriously. I married the most amazing man who has dedicated so much time to helping me blossom into my true self. Then I was lucky enough to meet *another* incredible man who gave me and my husband something we didn't even know we were missing, not to mention enabling us to leave jobs we were both only lukewarm about to have this awesome career.

Now I get bloody *paid* to let my gorgeous men fuck me all the time, and we have legions of adoring fans across the world. Companies pay us to sponsor their products, and occasionally we even fly around the globe to do that. And in my downtime, I get this unbelievable garden to potter about in and tend to.

I am one lucky boy.

But something shifted last night, and we can all feel it.

I know Papa well enough to tell without asking him like I did last night, but there's a needy part of me that had to hear it from him out loud. I haven't felt insecure like that for years, not since he coaxed my confidence out of me.

But that's just the thing. I know Papa *adores* doting on sweet, gentle boys, and we don't get to play with them often. Hell, I don't think Cundall has sent us anyone like that for at least the past two years. I think he reckons that kind of content won't do as well as the feisty gym bunnies that bounce in here, challenge Daddy, get fucked, fuck me, then bounce back out again.

But I'm not so sure now.

I'm very keen to see how Papa edits the footage we have so far together and then what the viewing figures are like. Because it *felt* electric. More than that, I felt like I immediately made a friend in Goldie. I know it's stupid, like I'm back at school thinking the first other little boy I speak to is going to be my best friend forever. But…well, that's how it feels.

Goldie is sweet and shy, but he seems to like my excitable energy that I know pisses a lot of our other playmates off. More than once, I've felt like our guests have tried to push me aside to try and get more of Daddy's attention. Of course Papa and Daddy *never* let me feel excluded. In fact, the second Daddy gets a whiff of that kind of vibe, he usually makes the playmate fuck me for him, and I love it because that's what Daddy wants.

But for the first time in as long as I can remember, I find myself wanting to play with someone for my own sake. In fact, I could even envisage *topping* Goldie if Daddy and Papa would like it. I think I'd like it.

I wiggle my toes. After this morning's scene, Goldie fell right back to sleep. Apparently, that's what he does after sex. I think it's fucking cute, but it was also seriously hot when Daddy didn't let him earlier and made him suck us all off. I could see how excited Goldie was, plus—*hello?* I'm not going to complain about having his pretty mouth on my chubby dick any time.

I was wide awake, though, so after a shower, I'd helped Papa prepare a breakfast feast like we always do for guests. Except this time, I'd taken extra care to cut the fruit up neatly and arrange everything so it looks even fancier than normal. I'd even gone and got some wildflowers from the garden to put in a slim vase.

I want Goldie to know that he was special. That whoever he'll work with after us should know he has fucking standards of care.

I sip my tea and frown, not liking the way I feel when I consider that Goldie's only just getting started and is no doubt going to have a stunning career in adult entertainment. I feel like a bratty kid, not wanting to share my toys. I understand I'll have to, but…well, I don't have to be happy about it.

That's one of the perks of being a brat. I'm allowed to pout.

Daddy's been in his office for a while and Papa went to do an early edit of one or two of the scenes. Usually, he waits until our guests are gone to do that, and I smirk to myself. He's like a kid at Christmas who can't wait to play with his new toy. I bet the footage of us four is *sensational.*

So I'm the only one who hears Goldie's voice as he enters the kitchen behind me. "Um, hello?"

I jump up from where I've been sitting and whirl around,

feeling the beaming smile on my face. Goldie looks freshly showered and is dressed in a plain red T-shirt and jeans with slightly damp hair. He still looks delectable, and I suspect he'd be gorgeous in anything.

"Morning, Goldie!" I cry as I bound over to him for a hug. He seems surprised at first, then leans into me and rubs my back. *Ahhh.* "Did you have a nice post-shag nap?" I ask with a wink.

He blushes, but I just giggle until he relaxes. "Um, yes, thank you."

"Are you hungry?" I indicate my and Papa's hard work. There's a big pot of porridge keeping warm on the hob that I've only just helped myself to, but I know it'll be scrummy, because that's how Papa makes it. There are also bowls of several types of fruit, chocolate chips, bottles of honey and other sauces, as well as fresh juice and croissants.

Goldie's eyes go wide. "You didn't do this because of me?" he whispers.

"Well, yeah," I say proudly. "Obviously, we'll all eat some —Daddy's very strict about food and keeping our strength up. But this is a special big breakfast because you're here."

He bites his lip and—*oh no*—looks upset! I can't have that.

"Goldie, what's wrong?" I ask, taking his hand and looking into his wet eyes. "Would you like something different? I can make toast, or there's cereal or—"

"No, no," he says urgently, shaking his head. "It's not that. I just…I feel bad that you made a fuss. All of you have already been more than kind, and I feel selfish for all this special treatment."

I feel so sad I don't know what to say for a moment. "But you *are* special," I tell him. I wanted to make him happy. I would never have dreamed that making breakfast would hurt his feelings. I hate that he doesn't think he deserves to be spoiled.

"What's going on here?" Papa's warm voice floats through the air, and I immediately relax. Papa will know how to make everything better.

"Goldie's worried that we've put ourselves out by making breakfast, but I was trying to tell him that we *wanted* to."

Goldie blinks back the tears, and I squeeze his hand as he looks over at Papa. "I'm not worth all this fuss. I'm sorry."

Papa raises his eyebrows and steps closer. He's got a bowl of porridge in his hand that he places on the large wooden table that dominates the centre of the kitchen.

"Now, Goldie," he says firmly as he cups the side of Goldie's face. "Who's in charge in this house?"

"Daddy," he replies immediately.

Papa beams at him. "That's right, good boy. So if Daddy told Baby and me to make sure you had a hearty breakfast and to keep you all cosy and taken care of whilst he does some work, do you think Daddy is wrong?"

I watch as Goldie bites his lips and frowns in thought. "No, I guess not."

Papa caresses his cheek. "Exactly. You don't need to worry about us making too much of a fuss or taking up our time, golden angel. That's for Daddy to decide. And if he wants to spoil his sweet boy—or all his boys—that's up to him, isn't it?"

"Yes," Goldie says with slightly more conviction.

Papa leans down and presses a chaste kiss to Goldie's mouth, and I feel the last of his tension ebbing away. I smile and bring his hand up to kiss the knuckles as well. "See? Everything is perfect. So can I get you some breakfast? You must be starving after all the fun we've been having." After all, he skipped dinner last night as he was too shattered.

"Um, yes," he says with a sigh of relief. "I am hungry, thank you. And the porridge smells amazing."

I lead him to the kitchen table to sit down, then nip out to the sun lounge to grab my untouched bowl of porridge. I've put strawberries in it as well as chocolate chips, which have melted a little, so it looks absolutely perfect now. I settle next to Goldie as Papa places a steaming bowl of fresh porridge down in front of him before fetching his own that he came in with.

Tentatively Goldie picks up a spoon and scoops up a heap of hot oats, but as he places his lips to it, he flinches away. "Sorry. Too hot," he quickly apologises.

Papa chuckles. "I have to let mine go completely cold, so I get you. Maybe you should let it cool down a while?"

"Or," I say eagerly, shoving my bowl his way, "why don't you try mine? I bet it's just right."

"But you already made it the way you like," Goldie says with a frown. "I couldn't take it from you."

"Don't you like strawberries and chocolate?" I ask. He might not. Papa and Daddy only put banana or blueberries in theirs, after all.

But he shakes his head. "No, I love strawberries and chocolate, but—"

"Perfect," I exclaim and swap our bowls. "See? I'll just make another one and eat it in a minute. I already had a croissant, so I'm not as starving as you must be."

Goldie opens his mouth, possibly to protest. But then he looks at Papa watching him and smiles, hopefully recalling the conversation they just had.

"Thank you, Baby," Goldie says to me. "That's really kind of you."

"Good boy," Papa says, rubbing his knee under the table.

I grin. "You're very welcome, Goldie. Now, is there anything else you'd like to add to it?"

He considers a moment, then squeezes in a good swirl of honey in before trying another bite. He sighs. "Just right," he announces.

I happily busy myself making another bowl and take inspiration from Goldie by adding honey along with strawberries and chocolate chips. It'll be too hot for another few minutes, so whilst the chocolate melts, I sip some orange juice and watch Goldie finish his whole bowl.

"That was amazing, thank you," he says to us, accepting the juice Papa poured for him as well. He looks shyly between us. "Can I, um, ask you a question?"

"Of course, Goldie," Papa says. He's also finished his porridge, and I tuck into mine as Goldie chews his lip and seems to consider his words. The chocolate melts on my tongue, and I resist the urge to groan.

"How did you meet Daddy?"

Warmth fills me, and Papa beams. "Ah, good question. We met him at a kink club." He reaches out for my hand and twists my wedding ring, making me feel all warm and gooey. "We were so happy, just the two of us. I love taking care of Baby so much, but there was a part of me that craved to be dominated sexually as well. I was afraid to tell Baby at first, but he's a brat, so he got it out of me eventually."

I laugh happily and kiss the back of his hand. "I love that you were brave enough to be honest with me, Papa. It made me feel so loved."

"I was worried he'd feel like he wasn't enough," Papa says with a sigh. "But I should have trusted my wonderful husband better. So we started going to kink clubs to find big tough Doms to play with, but it was only ever for the scenes. I thought that was enough—that was all we needed."

"Then we met Daddy," I interject, bouncing in my seat.

Papa nods, then drops his head back and laughs. "He marched right over to us and informed us that we were going home with him. Baby was cheeky and said he wasn't the boss of us."

I shudder at the memory of how his eyes smouldered. "He

pinched my chin and said yes he bloody was and that I was a naughty boy who needed a good spanking." And good it was. *So* good.

"We decided to take him up on his offer," Papa says with a grin. "Just for one night."

"That became a weekend. That became…" I use my hand to indicate the home and the life that we've built together.

"That's so romantic," Goldie says wistfully. "But you aren't married to him?"

Papa shakes his head. "That's not possible in the UK. Not yet," he adds firmly. He's passionate that one day the law will change for polyamorous people. "But we had a beautiful commitment ceremony that was essentially a wedding, and our finances are all properly set up so our bank accounts and the cottage are in all three of our names, should anything happen to one of us."

I whimper because I *hate* thinking about anything bad happening to Papa or Daddy. But it's sensible to make sure these things are sorted, so I signed everything they told me to. It makes me happy to know that the three of us are protected.

Papa stands up to hug me and kiss my head, calming me back down. "Nothing bad is going to happen," he assures me. "Everything is okay."

"Of course it is. Why wouldn't it be?"

"Daddy!" I squeal happily as he enters the kitchen as well. I gasp. "And Princess, yay!"

I jump up to pet our enormous ginger tabby cat that Daddy has lying on her back in his grasp. She's so big she still looks huge even in Daddy's thick arms. A lot of cats don't like their bellies being touched, but Princess practically demands it. She purrs loudly, and I turn to see what Goldie thinks of her.

His eyes are comically wide, and his mouth is in a pretty O-shape. "You have a cat?" he whispers. "May I say hello?"

"Of course," I cry, keen to show her off. "We've had her four years, and she's a darling."

"She's a lazy little madam," Daddy says, but his tone is all syrupy. He was adamant he didn't like cats until I'd pulled a brat card and Papa and I adopted her anyway. I swear Daddy loves her the most of all of us.

Goldie approaches carefully before slowly putting his hand out. When Princess doesn't scratch him, he tries petting her, his face lighting up like a Christmas tree when her purring resumes.

"Mum and I aren't allowed pets in our flat," he says, and my interest piques at the mention of his life back home. So he lives with his mum? "We'd absolutely love one, though. I'm always making friends with cats on the street. She does too when she can get out and about."

I share a glance with Papa. That sounds like his mum is sick or maybe has mobility issues. If Goldie is caring for her, does that mean he's come into adult entertainment to support her? The money is great in porn, for sure. But that's not a good reason to do it. Your heart needs to be in it.

I see Daddy frowning at Goldie, too, and I know he's thinking the same. I'm normally the one being taken care of, but in that moment, even I feel my protective hackles rise. I'm of the very firm opinion that the three of us need to do a really good job of looking after Goldie whilst he's here.

And to be honest, with us all crowding around Princess as she laps up our fussing, it seems so natural and right for the three of us to huddle around Goldie, touching his back and kissing his hair.

I make it my mission there and then to help him understand how special he is before the weekend is done.

And maybe even beyond this weekend. Who knows?

GOLDIE

THE NEXT TWO DAYS GO BY FAR TOO QUICKLY. AFTER breakfast on Saturday, Baby showed me the gardens where he spends a lot of his free time. I have killed any houseplants I've tried to tend to, so his green thumb is especially impressive to me. But more than that, I love how his whole face shines with pride when he talks about something he loves. Whether that be his flowerbeds, Princess, or his Papa and Daddy.

After lunch, we did a photoshoot around the cottage. Baby offered that I could borrow one of his cartoony T-shirts. I'd never be brave enough to wear something so bold, but when he insisted and Daddy nodded in approval, I allowed the decision to be taken out of my hands, and it felt *wonderful.* Baby picked out a My Little Pony top for me, and I have to say I think I looked kind of cute in it.

Maybe I wouldn't normally wear something like that, but *Goldie* does. And he loved it.

The scenes started off sort of innocent, but then we were quickly down to our underwear. Daddy provided me with some brand-new briefs from a company they were promoting, and he told me to get myself a little hard before squeezing myself into them. That wasn't difficult. I've pretty much been half-hard since I walked through the bloody door.

The photos had gotten raunchier after that, naturally segueing into more sex. Blow jobs, frotting, hand jobs, toys, and all kinds of anal play. It had been a wild afternoon of mind-blowing fun. Then that evening…we'd snuggled.

I'd almost been a little miffed to begin with. I know I'm feeling precious about how little time I'm going to have with these three men, and I have to stop making myself sad by counting down the hours. But Daddy had asked Baby to put on a film whilst Papa made us a vat of pasta and a rich tomatoey meat sauce. Their sofa is enormous, so all four of us cuddled under blankets watching the fun action film Baby had picked out.

I'd slept in their private bed again that night, staying away from the room I knew so well from all the films I've watched and now from the elaborate scenes we've done in there. There were still plenty of orgasms to go around before we fell asleep, but it had been the sleepy kind under the blankets. No role playing. Just tender words and hot, possessive touches.

Baby had nudged me awake on Sunday morning, asking if I wanted to surprise Papa and Daddy the same way he'd surprised me on Saturday morning. My heart had thundered in my chest with nerves and thrilling excitement, not quite believing I was daring to wake Daddy up with a blow job he hadn't asked for. But as he'd stirred to life, his hand had gripped my hair, tugging me farther down his length. Before he was even fully awake, he'd moaned how good and perfect and greedy I was.

I'd loved every second of it.

Papa had made us a full English for brunch with creamy

scrambled eggs, crunchy hash browns, sliced avocado, and juicy bacon, all smothered with hot baked beans and lashings of tomato ketchup. He'd winked as he'd served it up, saying we'd be needing our strength.

He hadn't been wrong.

Now it's Sunday evening, and I feel like we've been fucking for hours. Daddy had let me come first for once, I suspect because he wants me to come again after they'd all claimed me. To start with, they'd laid me down on the thick, fluffy rug with the crackling fireplace in the living room, cameras pointed at me from all directions as they'd licked and kissed and stroked every inch of me until I'd come all over my belly in a quivering mess.

I haven't even seen any of the footage of myself yet. I kind of don't want to. I feel strangely calm about the idea of thousands of strangers seeing me at my most intimate and vulnerable. But if I were to watch anything back, raw or edited together, I think it would remind me that this isn't *real*. It might feel real with just the four of us in this house, away from the real world. However, the truth is that this is just a means to an end. A way to clear my debt and earn my freedom from Robert, Mr. Cundall, and all of Honipot.

But I've read too many romance novels. My heart keeps trying to look for signs that this is more than that for Daddy, Papa, and Baby. Except I *know* this is just work for them. They'll make the next guy they play with feel like it's real, too. That's why they're the best. It's their job to make people believe that what they see on screen is love.

So it's a good thing Daddy is here to claim me and make all my decisions for me, keeping me delirious so I can't worry about what will happen this time tomorrow when I'm back in London in my small, cold flat, far away from this beautiful cottage and the gorgeous men who live here.

Baby topped me for the first time. He sweetly asked if

that would be okay and if I'd like it. He said he never usually tops, but he hoped it would be okay if Papa fucked him at the same time. I love it when Daddy tells me how it's going to be, but there was something really special about Baby asking like that. Of course I said I'd love it, and they'd had me bent over the sofa in no time.

Baby came in me, but Papa held off. He allowed Baby and me a few minutes as Baby softened inside me whilst we kissed and giggled together. Then Papa got me back on the rug on all fours to take his time pounding my arse. By this point in the weekend, I'm undeniably sore, but I'll be damned if I'm going to say anything. I only have mere hours left in this blissful bubble, and I refuse to squander them.

Daddy had watched Baby and then Papa ravishing me, his monster cock hard in his hand as he leisurely stroked himself, his eyes dark with lust. By the time Papa drops his head back and gnashes his teeth through his orgasm, I'm trembling, sweating, rock hard, and all my worries have melted away.

That's when Daddy comes to sit on the rug with me, the light from the flames dancing over his huge body, all the dark hair casting little shadows on his skin. He props himself up with one hand resting behind his arse. The other he uses to take my hip and guide him onto his dick. I'm better at taking him now and feel good and stretched from Baby and Papa. I straddle his hips and ride him, holding on to his strong shoulders, gazing into his dark and stormy eyes.

As he blows his load inside me, kissing my neck and rasping that I'm perfect, I wish this moment would last forever. I'm full of the cum of these three men. Daddy holds me as Papa holds Baby on the rug beside us, drinking in every second of our show. I still need to come—my cock is painful now—but I almost don't want to. It's Sunday evening, and this will probably be our last big scene. If I don't come, I can stay in this moment forever.

But then Daddy eases out of me. I lie down on my front with Papa and Baby on either side of me, cuddling close. I grind my cock into the thick rug, chasing release as they touch and kiss my skin and Daddy eats out their mixed cum from my arse, murmuring how sweet and delicious all his boys are.

I don't realise I'm sobbing until Daddy rolls me over and pulls me into his lap, kissing the tears away and shushing me in a soothing voice.

"Do you think you can stand, golden angel?" he asks me, brushing my damp hair from my forehead. "You've been so very good for your Daddy and deserve a special treat."

I take a few shaky breaths, blinking tears away from my eyes. "Yes, Daddy," I whisper. I'm tempted to say that I don't need a reward, that being with Daddy and Papa and Baby is enough of a treat. But I'm greedy and want to take everything I can get from these wonderful men whilst I can still pretend that they're mine.

He helps steady me on the rug, then moves behind me as Papa and Baby kneel at my feet. "Just relax, sweet boy," Daddy says as he nuzzles against my cheeks, nipping and kissing them. "We're here to worship you."

His tongue finds my swollen, tender hole again. Papa sucks the tip of my leaking cock, and Baby takes my heavy balls into his mouth. I shudder, gasp, and cry, only just managing to stop my knees from buckling as I move my hands, running my fingers through Daddy's and Papa's hair and over Baby's buzz cut.

I feel powerful standing over them as they use their mouths to worship me, but safe because I know Daddy is in charge and calling all the shots. It's a heady kind of bliss, and I find myself floating away for a little while, even though I'd been so desperate before to come. However, it's not long before I can feel my climax rising, and I whimper as it begins to crest.

Daddy leaves my hole to move around the front, easing between Papa and Baby, who both pop off me. The three of them kneel before me, and my breath hitches at such a magnificent sight.

"That's it, golden angel," Daddy says as he pumps my cock. "Come for us. You're so beautiful."

"Daddy," I whine, leaning on his shoulders for support as my legs have gone to jelly. I manage to keep my eyes open a sliver so I can peek through my eyelashes. I *need* to be looking at them as I come.

Then…oh *fuck.* Papa and Baby lean in, kissing and licking my head as Daddy continues to jerk me. It's too much. I can't hold on any longer.

I paint Papa and Baby's faces as long, white ropes start spurting out. The streams hit Daddy's hairy chest as I gasp, my own chest heaving and my world blacking out. The only reason I manage to stay standing is because I'm gripping Daddy's shoulders so hard that I'm going to leave bruises.

Eventually, I'm spent, and Daddy yanks me down to collapse in his lap. I'm being peppered with kisses from all three of them as he holds me tight, and I hum in contentment.

As usual, sleep tries its best to claim me, but we are suddenly interrupted by a hard banging on the door. I feel all three of my men stiffen, their heads snapping towards the front of the cottage. They have a very clear 'no soliciting' sign on the front gate and no neighbours for miles.

"Who could that be?" Baby asks.

I don't know, but I'm wide awake again. I don't want anyone to intrude on our blissful little bubble, especially when come tomorrow morning, it will be gone forever.

"It's probably just a courier delivery or something," Papa says cheerfully.

Daddy scowls and grabs a box of tissues off the coffee table. "Whoever they are, they can piss off," he says as he begins to wipe my cum off Papa's and Baby's faces and necks, then off his own chest. As Papa stands to fetch the dressing gowns we'd left out of shot, Baby hops up to switch off the various cameras. Daddy hugs me tightly and kisses my hair, glaring at the door as if daring them to knock again.

They do. It's louder this time, and it doesn't stop.

Daddy snarls as he moves me from his lap, climbs to his feet, and snatches the biggest dressing gown from Papa as he hands them all out. "This better be fucking good," Daddy gripes as he storms through the archway dividing the living room from the entrance hall towards the door.

I only just get my robe on in time before he flicks the locks and yanks the door open. "What?" he barks at the person waiting on the other side. Clearly, he doesn't recognise him.

But I do.

"Robert?" I whisper in disbelief.

DADDY

"Who's Robert?" I growl.

I rip my eyes away from the wanker who has dared darken my door to look at Goldie, but...oh *shit*. He's gone as white as a sheet, his wide eyes tearing up, and he's trembling. I snap my head back to the bloke in front of me, but he's used my moment of distraction to slip inside the house.

My house.

"Babe," he cries, flinging his arms open. He's not as big as me, but compared to Goldie, he's broad and tall, with scruffy hair and an even scruffier beard. Ill-fitting jeans and a tatty bomber jacket make for an all-over poor impression. "It's been a while."

"W-what are you doing here?" Goldie splutters, and I'm pleased that Papa puts his hands protectively on his shoulders because I'm not moving from this dickhead's side. I *will* bodily remove him from my property if needs be. But not before I get some bloody answers.

"Who are you, and how did you get this address?" I demand.

He rolls his eyes and indicates Goldie with his hand. "I'm

this tasty treat's boyfriend," he says like I'm a dumb fuck for not knowing that. "And Cundall gave me the address because I was worried, babe. What have you gotten yourself into?"

Cundall did *what?* I'm going to wring his fucking neck.

"*Ex*-boyfriend!" Goldie squeaks, much to my relief. I've known plenty of adult entertainers in relationships, but I would have been pissed off if Goldie hadn't admitted that to us.

And, okay, yeah, the idea that he belonged to someone else did *not* impress me. I don't care that this weekend is work. I know what's mine when I see it.

"Babe," Robert scoffs. "Don't be like that."

"I *broke up* with you!" Goldie cries. "After...you know what!"

I narrow my eyes and glare at this prick. I don't know what happened to make Goldie dump his arse, but I sorely want to.

"If Goldie says you're his ex, you're his ex," Papa says firmly.

Baby hugs both Papa and Goldie. Bless my baby boy. He may be my sweet bratty sub, but he's not a coward. I see in his eyes the determination to put himself between our golden angel and this twat.

Luckily, he doesn't have to worry about that because his Daddy is here.

"Goldie?" Robert mocks. "You let these fucknuts name you?"

I move myself between my men and our unwanted guest. "Why did Cundall give you our private home address that you were *certainly* not invited to?" I ask, keeping my voice low but even.

Robert looks me up and down like he's unimpressed. He's either stupid or monumentally arrogant. I'm willing to bet it's both.

"Old Cunny showed me the footage you fellows sent him yesterday. Reckoned I wanted to see how my babe had moved up in the world."

Even though that's against protocol, I'm not surprised Cundall would violate our privacy agreement like that. He's always on the lookout for drama.

Robert shakes his head and turns back to Goldie. "I gotta say, you've been holding out on me. You're a right little slut, aren't you? All 'Daddy' this and begging for it like you haven't had a decent shag in your life."

I bet he hasn't. Not from this douchebag, anyway.

I startle him by grabbing his worn jacket and lifting him onto his toes. "Did you just call one of my men a slut?" I ask in a dangerously cheery tone.

Finally, the prick has the good sense to look scared. Unfortunately, his mouth is still running.

"You're fucking *porn* stars!" he yells, spittle flying on my face. "This isn't who my babe is! I came to rescue him, to take him home where he *belongs.*"

"I'm not going anywhere with you!" Goldie shouts.

I grin at Robert, feeling like a feral beast. "Hear that? You're shit outta luck."

Robert smacks at my hands, and I release him but only to shove him towards the door. "This place stinks of sex," Robert hisses. "Babe, they're just using you. None of this is real. Come home with me! Now I know what you can really do, I know it could be amazing between us!"

"If you didn't realise Goldie is amazing from the *second* you laid eyes on him," I snarl, "then you don't fucking deserve him." But I make myself grit my teeth. This shit is important, even though I fucking hate having to ask it. "However, this is Goldie's decision. Goldie, do you want to leave with this man?"

He's more of a rat than a man, but I need to make sure

Goldie gives an honest answer. I can tell this fucker to piss off, but it will be easier if he's heard it from Goldie's own mouth that he's not interested.

At least, I hope. I hope Robert will listen to reason.

And I hope to *God* that Goldie doesn't want to go with such a slimeball.

I should never have doubted my golden angel, though.

"No!" he shrieks. "No, Daddy, I don't want to go with him! I want to stay here with you!" But then his face falls, and his chin trembles. "Do I have to…do you want me to leave?"

"No!" Baby shouts in the time it takes me to whirl around and grab Goldie's head so he can look into my eyes.

"You are *mine*," I say, my heart racing. "So long as you want to stay, I am not letting you out of my sight. Do you understand?"

I'll be brutally honest—if he'd have said he wanted to go, I would have picked him up and not let him go until he explained *why* he would do something so foolish. Luckily, it doesn't come to that.

He relaxes and nods against my hands. "Yes, Daddy," he sobs. "Thank you so much."

"Oh, give me a fucking *break*," Robert snaps. I look over to see him throw his hands in the air. *"Daddy, Daddy, Daddy.* Do you realise how pathetic you sound? Babe, *none of this is real."* He punctuates those last five words each with a smack of his hands together. "You're not like them! They fuck for *money.* You're better than that!"

"These men are a hundred times the man you are!" Goldie whimpers, clinging to all three of us. "You *work* for Honipot. Why do you always look down on the talent? This is why your film failed!"

Pride wells in my chest at how brave my golden angel is being, but I didn't miss the part where this twat works for Cundall.

After this gross invasion of privacy, I'll be seeing what I can do about both of their jobs. But for now, I've had enough.

"Fuck off out of my house," I say calmly, turning back to my men. This wanker is no threat to me, but he is getting on my tits now. "Goldie is ours. I doubt you were ever worthy of him."

"You *owe* me!" Robert shouts at Goldie, his tone finally dropping all those fake niceties. "You were *never* that good to me! I deserve a piece of that arse! And if you're whoring yourself out now, why do you even care? It's not like you have standards. I should make you get over here and suck my dick right now. I bet you'd get off on that, you filthy little—"

I can't stop myself. I'm spinning around, and my fist is connecting with his face before I even think twice. He pinwheels, crashing into the chest of drawers in the entrance hall and sending a vase of flowers smashing to the ground.

I'd had no idea that Princess had been hiding underneath the drawers. She comes hurtling out, her claws scrabbling on the floorboards. She shoots past me and my men, diving under the coffee table before hissing loudly at Robert.

"You tell him, Princess," Baby cries. "Fuck off, you tosser," he shouts at Robert. "Nobody wants you here!"

Robert rubs his bloody lip. "This isn't over," he threatens Goldie.

I'm opening my mouth, ready to tell him yet again to fuck off before I haul him out of the front door.

But then Goldie is screaming.

I turn in horror as tears stream down his face. He draws breath, his gaze filled with fury and such bitter sadness. *"I hate you!"* he bellows, straining against Papa, who is holding him back. "You ruined my life. You're *nothing!* I'm never going back to you, never ever *ever!* You're the reason I'm even here in the first place! You're nothing to me, so get out! *Get out! Get out! GET OUT!"*

I want to scoop him up in my arms and protect him from the entire *world.* But first I have to make him safe again.

So I march over to the weasel that has dared come to *my* home and threaten *my* boy, grab him by the scruff of his neck, and physically *throw* him out the front door. He yelps as he rolls arse over tit along the gravel pathway, ending up on the grass. He scrambles to his feet, spluttering indignantly, but I jab a finger at him in the dark.

"Get off my *fucking* property right now, and I won't call the police. Stick around, and maybe I can show your balls how good I am with my nine iron."

"You sick fuck," he wails. "You can't have him! He's *mine!* Not for some dirty porno but real love! Babe! Come out here!"

I sneer at him, turn around, and slam the door. I'm serious about both the police and the golf club, but I'd really rather not waste another second on that vile creep.

All I care about are my men.

I pause for a second, my heart breaking. Goldie has slumped to the floor and is sobbing his heart out. Baby clings to him, as does Papa, who looks up desperately at me.

"I'm sorry," Goldie is whispering, his eyes screwed up like he's trying to make himself disappear. "I'm so, *so* sorry."

Well, this won't do at all.

GOLDIE

I KNEW THIS FAIRY TALE HAD TO BE TOO GOOD TO BE TRUE. Reality had come crashing through the door—literally—and now my whole world is shattering.

"I'm s-sorry. I'm so sorry," I keep stuttering. I'm vaguely aware of arms around me, of being held, but I can't stay in this cocoon. "I'll go. I'll leave. I'm so *sorry.*"

A rough hand pinches my chin, and I blink through watery lashes at Daddy as his fierce gaze pierces at me. I flinch away, screwing my eyes shut again, dread washing through me.

"I'm sorry, Daddy!" I squeak. "It's all my fault!"

"Golden angel, you have nothing to be sorry for," he says. However, I can't really hear him. The words skim over me like a stone on a pond. "Please look at me."

But I can't stop crying. There's a loud whistling rushing through my head, and I can't seem to catch my breath.

Mr. Cundall told Robert this address. He must have wanted him to come here. But there was no *way* I was going to leave with him. Fear and revulsion rip through me, and I

89

quake. The things he said, the way he talked about forcing himself on me...

I swoon, feeling sick, only held up by Papa's and Baby's embrace. I can't believe I ever let such a disgusting, snivelling man touch me.

But I did. Because I'm weak and can't do anything by myself. He'd promised to take care of me, but he didn't. He'd ruined me. And now...

I gasp, a fresh wave of dizziness surging through me as my sore eyes snap open. I think Daddy is talking, but I can't hear him.

Will Mr. Cundall be angry? Will he cancel our deal?

No...no, surely, the footage we've recorded will still make him the money back. I held up my end of the bargain. But... what if he wants me to do more work with Robert? I try and remember if Robert just said anything like that, but everything is so jumbled.

I've ruined *everything*. Things were so perfect with Daddy and Papa and Baby. I've loved this weekend with them. It's quite possibly been the best couple of days of my whole life. But then Robert showed up to start a fight over me, and things got broken, and Princess was scared, and they probably *hate* me now for giving their address away. Because of me, Robert invaded their sanctuary.

"I'm sorry," I hear myself whimpering in a far-off way, like someone else is speaking the words I'm thinking. "I'll leave." I almost beg them to forgive me, but that's not fair on them.

I've lied to them about why I'm here. I brought a menace into their home. I was greedy and made them run around after me without lifting a finger. I tried to help with chores, but they wouldn't let me, but I should have tried *harder*. I'm selfish and useless and—

"GOLDIE!"

I feel like I've been doused with a bucket of cold water. My sight and hearing suddenly come roaring back. Daddy's face is still in front of mine, his fingers gripping my chin. But where I saw anger before, I now see concern.

My breathing is ragged. "D-Daddy?" I whisper. How long has he been trying to get me to snap out of my downward spiral? I gasp for air as if I'd been struggling to get my head above water.

For the first time I've ever seen, Daddy's face truly softens. He caresses the side of my face and wraps his other hand around the back of my neck, holding tightly, like an anchor. "Sweet boy," he says. "Good boy. You've done absolutely nothing wrong, so I need you to stop apologising. And I *definitely* need you to stop talking about leaving, okay? That's not allowed. We agreed until tomorrow morning, didn't we?"

I nod, my head clearer. I wrestle with my heart, but I try and see the positive. The contract is only until tomorrow morning. That's true. But Daddy still wants me until then. I don't have to give up this fantasy just yet.

I still feel guilty, though. "But Robert—"

"He's gone, angel," Daddy interrupts. "You'll never have to see him again, I promise. Daddy told him you aren't his, and you never were."

"You're *ours*," Baby insists, burying his face against my neck. I feel Papa stroking my hair.

It's not real. It's only until tomorrow morning. But for now, I cling to the illusion like a life raft.

Oh, *fuck!* I wish this was real! I wish I could stay! But it's just a job. Daddy, Papa, and Baby don't want me interfering with their relationship. We made an agreement, and I'll stick to it.

I just have to hope that if I do everything to the letter, Mr. Cundall will still forgive my debt.

I wish—

Daddy's lips crash onto mine, his strong hands clutching at my jaw. "Goldie," he growls against my lips. "Stop worrying. Stop thinking altogether. It's Daddy's job to make all the decisions, isn't it?"

"Y-yes," I answer.

He can still be my Daddy for now. Just for a few more hours. So I let my eyes flutter closed, thinking only about the way his hands feel clutching on to my face.

"Yes, what?" he asks.

"Yes, Daddy," I say quickly. Against my better judgement, I open my eyes again, fear lodging in my throat. "Do you really still want me? Even after I've been so bad?"

Daddy's nostrils flare. "Did Daddy say you were bad?"

I open and close my mouth. "N-no, but—"

"Are you calling Daddy a liar?" he demands, and I hastily shake my head. "Good. Because Daddy actually said that you were his good, perfect, *sweet* boy. None of what just happened was your fault. *None* of it. Daddy thought you were brave, and he's so proud of you for saying what you want, for staying strong. Do you understand me, golden angel?"

I bite my lip. I *know* Daddy knows best, and he's certainly not a liar. But I can't fully make these awful feelings go away. I don't deserve all this love and patience.

Love? It's not love. It's not real. It's—

Daddy growls and suddenly puts his huge arms around me, picking me up as he stands. I squeak and hastily wrap myself around him like a koala. He sighs and rubs the short hairs at the back of my neck, sending shivers down my spine.

"All my gorgeous boys in the shower now, please," he says softly.

As he walks down the corridor, I look over his shoulder at Papa and Baby following us hand in hand. Baby meets my gaze, then scuttles forward a few steps to reach up and cup the side of my face. I take a shuddery breath, but some of the bad thoughts are drifting away.

Now, if I can just keep them away.

We reach the bathroom, and Daddy gets the water going before he even puts me down. Steam starts filling the air as he settles me. Then one by one, he takes each of our robes off. Even Papa's as he's comforting Baby. Papa looks up as Daddy slips the thick robe off his shoulders, leaning up to press a chaste kiss to his lips.

"Thank you, Daddy," he murmurs.

Guilt and fear threaten to creep back into my mind, but then Daddy gently steers me under the water along with Papa and Baby, and then we're all hugging together under the scorching hot stream.

I close my eyes and let it consume me, the steam filling my lungs whilst the blistering water pounds down, making my skin tingle. Three solid bodies press against me, hands rubbing slowly up and down my back, chest, and arms. I feel a kiss on my temple, then another from the other side. Every inch of me is being touched or held by the water or by my lovers.

I know I can't keep all the bad thoughts away for long. They're too real, too heavy. But right now, I can choose to succumb to them, or I can choose to be present for the last few precious hours I have with these incredible men. They are a gift I shall treasure forever.

It feels like I can't imagine life without them, but that's just because this weekend has been so intense. I'm sure that after a few days back in my normal life, I'll be okay. I've survived before, and I'll survive again.

So I focus only on their gentle touches and possessive lips. Daddy washes all three of us, and I allow myself to lean against his broad, furry chest as he pays special attention to my intimate areas, making sure I'm thoroughly clean after our scene this afternoon.

I don't want to leave the comfort of the shower, but my fingers are getting pruney. Daddy must realise that because he turns off the water and wraps us in a big, fluffy white towel each. Papa begins to help Baby dry, but Daddy shakes his head.

"No, my love. Come here."

I watch as Daddy rubs his hands against Papa's arms through the towel, and for a second, Papa sobs, screwing his eyes shut. Then he lets out a shaky breath, opens his eyes, nods with a small smile, and kisses Daddy gently on the mouth.

Then they both turn to Baby, who smiles and sighs happily as they give him a quick dry.

Then it's my turn.

Now they all have their towels wrapped around their hips, so their hands are free to move my towel against all parts of my body. The steam is clearing, and although it's getting a little colder, I focus solely on the way the material feels against my skin, basking in the fact that all three of my men are tending to me after the horrible shock of Robert appearing out of nowhere.

Now I'm calmer, I'm starting to see that wasn't exactly my fault. Yes, Robert came looking for me, but I didn't ask him to, and I certainly wasn't the one to give him the cottage's address.

"Thank you, Daddy," I say.

His head snaps up, and I expect him to ask 'for what?' Instead, his smile is warm, and he just says, "Of course, sweet boy. Daddy knows what's best, and he'll *always* be there to take care of you and make the right choices. Okay?"

Well, not always, but at least for tonight. I swallow down the lump in my throat and manage a nod.

I don't want the evening to end, but as Daddy herds us into the bedroom like a flock of sheep, I can't help but yawn, exhaustion consuming me. I hear him chuckle warmly as he rubs my back.

"Time for bed, little ones," he says.

He arranges us naked under the covers so he's on the right-hand side, then me, Baby, and finally Papa on the left-hand side. Daddy and Papa cuddle us inwards, so Baby and I are wrapped up. Even if it's just a resting hand or a leg slung over, we're all touching each other in some way.

I try and fight sleep, not wanting this beautiful moment to end. But I can't stop time as it marches on regardless of my breaking heart. At least I get to spend one more night in this gorgeous cottage with these stunning men. Even Princess, the cat, hops onto the bed and curls up to sleep at our feet.

I tell myself I'm blessed to have had this time at all. I could have had to pay off Mr. Cundall's loan with men who were uncaring or mean. This has been the greatest privilege of my life.

And when it ends tomorrow, I won't be ungrateful.

I will treasure this time for as long as I live.

15

DADDY

I'M ONLY HALF-AWAKE, AND YET I KNOW SOMETHING IS WRONG.

My eyes snap open. Glancing at the clock, I see it's a little later than we'd normally sleep in, but that's to be expected after yesterday's upset.

What's *not* to be expected is the fact that I only have two of my three men in my bed.

I frown, telling myself that everything's more than likely fine. Goldie is probably just taking a piss. But worry gnaws at my gut, and it won't be sated until I see that my angel is okay. If he's gotten up early to think, he might need some cuddles from his Daddy to soothe him.

I still have so many questions from Robert's visit. Namely, what the hell had Goldie meant when he'd said that him being here was all Robert's fault? Had Robert made Goldie feel so inadequate in bed he'd turned to porn to prove him wrong?

At least I'm pretty sure where Goldie's insecurities about giving blow jobs and everything else came from. It sounded like that dickhead didn't appreciate a *fraction* of what Goldie is worth. I hated Goldie speaking that way about himself, and now I think it wasn't an act at all. He really did think he was rubbish in bed.

It makes me want to hit Robert all over again.

Except no, I don't. I don't care about such a mouth-breather. I care about my boys. So I leave Papa and Baby sleeping, throw on a pair of joggers, then go out to look for Goldie.

I'm met by Princess, who's lurking in the corridor. The door was ajar, so I'm not sure why she hasn't come in like she usually does. She had a hell of a fright last night and was on the bed at our feet every time I stirred in the night. But not now.

She wails at me.

"Shh, little one," I whisper. "Papa and Baby are sleeping. What is it?" I go to scoop her up, but she slips from my fingers, trotting down the hallway, giving another yell. I chuckle and follow her to the living room.

Where I stop laughing.

Goldie is sitting on the couch, dressed in the clothes he arrived in, his backpack resting by his feet. His phone is clutched in his hands, and he looks guiltily up at me as I stop in the entranceway.

"What's going on?" I ask, not jumping to conclusions. But my heart is thumping fast and my skin prickling.

Goldie's lip trembles, and he looks back down at his phone. "The weekend is over. The contract is up."

I swallow. I don't often get frightened of anything, but right now, he's scaring the shit out of me. I have to seriously fight the urge to shout at him and bodily bring him back to bed.

"Okay," I say evenly. "The contract for work is done, yes. But why is your bag packed?"

Princess butts her head against the rucksack and meows loudly at him. She sounds like how I feel.

Goldie swallows and doesn't look me in the eyes. "Thank you so much for such an incredible experience. You've all been so kind and—"

"What's going on?"

I turn around to see Papa and Baby in their dressing gowns behind me. It was Baby who spoke, and his eyes are wide.

"Goldie, where are you going?" he asks, a quiver in his voice.

Goldie bites his own lip. "This was a lot of fun, but I have to go back to my real life now. I folded your T-shirt up and left it in the bathroom hamper. Thank you for lending it to me. Mr. Cundall said this arrangement was just for the weekend, and I have to—"

"*Fuck* Cundall," I roar, finally releasing some of my fear and anger. "What is all this talk of leaving? I told you last night that you're staying here."

He screws his eyes shut, twin tears falling down his face. When he speaks, it's barely a whisper, and I can't believe what I'm hearing.

"That was when you were my Daddy."

Were?

"What the actual fuck?" I rasp. I feel Papa's hand on my shoulder, but I shrug it off. "What part of 'you're mine' was unclear? Did I *say* you could leave?"

A car horn honks outside, and Goldie chokes back a sob as he stands. "That's my taxi. I...I'm sorry. This has been the most amazing time, but I know it's not real, and I think I have to leave now before I ruin everything. I...thank you."

I can't believe what I'm witnessing. But then my rage takes over. Not real? What the fuck? Does he think it's like this with every man we fuck? Did it mean so little to him after all we went through? After every fucking thing I've said to him, he's telling me it really *was* just an act.

"Fine," I snap, looking at the wall rather than feel the betrayal further by looking into that angelic face one last time. "If it all meant nothing to you, fuck off."

I don't wait to see him walk out of the door. Instead, I march through the house until I reach the back door, where I shove my feet into a pair of boots and thrust my head into a jumper I'd left there some time ago. Slamming the door in my wake, I continue stomping over the bridge that crosses the stream, pretending I can't hear the car engine as it pulls away.

I don't come home for a long time.

I KNOW I'm still in a filthy fucking temper as the afternoon rolls around, so once I'm back home, I hide myself away from Papa and Baby in my office. They don't deserve my short fuse and thunderous mood.

But I just don't understand. It's so rare that I misread things. It's my job to look after my men and know what's best for them. Always.

Doesn't Goldie see that he needs me?

Apparently not.

I've told myself that I'm working on our finances, but really, I'm just angrily flicking between spreadsheets.

What kind of life has Goldie gone back to? Is it really so much better than being here with us? I remember him talking about his mum. I obviously don't expect him to abandon her, especially not when it sounded like she needs caring for.

But who's caring for *Goldie?* Call me presumptuous, but I'd assumed that was going to be my job from now on. When I'd told Papa and Baby they were mine, they'd just...*stayed.* It was probably foolish of me to think it would be the same with Goldie...but yeah, okay, maybe I did.

My stomach swoops unpleasantly, thinking of him continuing to work for Cundall. When I'm less murderous, I still fully intend on calling that useless prick up and asking him what the ever-loving fuck he was thinking in giving Robert our address. Not just that, though. I want to know Goldie's history and how he approached Cundall in the first place. What kind of contract has he got him on?

Because I know one thing for sure. As furious as I am with my golden angel, I know without a shadow of a doubt that I don't trust a single other fuck at that company to care for him properly. Not the way he needs or deserves. *I'm* the only one who can do that for him. He belongs *here*, with me, Papa, and Baby.

I refuse to accept that he doesn't want that. But he obviously feels a part of him doesn't deserve that, which only proves how much he needs his Daddy. I'd say he's going to get a hell of a punishment for disobeying me on this, but the truth is I'm so consumed with worry for his well-being I wouldn't lift a finger against him. Baby loves a good spanking. But Goldie needs wrapping in my arms so I can tell him everything's going to be okay. Daddy will make sure of it. He is *mine* to play with, to get the very best from him and make him shine like he's supposed to.

I squeeze my eyes shut, growling at the lump that threatens to rise in my throat. Emotions are fucking useless here. I need to act logically to fix this fuckery.

But I have to face the real possibility that our golden angel doesn't want anything fixed. Otherwise, why would he walk away so easily?

There's a knock at the door. "Fuck off," I snap. I'm not cross with my two boys at all, but I know myself, and I won't be able to stop myself from lashing out at them anyway. I am always in control, and I *hate* when that's taken away from me.

They don't listen. I grit my teeth as Papa enters with his open laptop in his arms, Baby walking by his side.

They both look far too fucking cheerful.

Have I lost my mind? Am I the only one who thought the four of us had something here? Why aren't they as devastated as I am?

"I said—"

"I heard you," Papa says calmly. He places his laptop on my desk, the screen facing him with its back to me. "We need to talk about Goldie."

"What's there to talk about?" I snap. "He came, he fucked, he got paid, he left. That was all it meant to him."

Baby still looks far too excited as he rocks on the balls of his feet. Papa raises his eyebrows and just looks at me for a few seconds. I can tell he's trying to get me to calm down, but I'm not fucking interested. Papa continues regardless.

"Actually, that's the thing."

"What is?"

He smirks at me. "That twat, Robert, isn't the only one who can wheedle information out of Cundall. After his spectacular fuck-up, I managed to convince him to tell me everything about Goldie."

I sometimes forget that my handsome man used to be a legal secretary. It's one of the reasons our business operations are so tight. He knows just the right things to say to make grown men piss themselves.

"So?" I ask in spite of myself. But I can't help it. As cross as I still am, I want to know everything about our sweet boy.

"So, he didn't get paid."

I shrug. *"Will* get paid," I grouse. "You know what I mean. This was just a job to him. No matter what we felt, he—"

"He isn't getting a *penny*, Daddy," Baby interjects. His fists are balled, and his excitement has morphed into distress. I'm guessing he and Papa have already discussed what Cundall had to say. "Do you remember when Goldie said to Robert that it was his fault Goldie was here?"

I do, but I just grunt in response. I'd been going over and over that. He'd made it sound like otherwise he'd never have come at my request.

Like he didn't even want to be here, when I'd thought he'd settled right in. I thought this was maybe meant to be his home, too.

"Robert works as a producer for Honipot," Papa explains, turning his laptop around to show me some roster or something. I don't care. I just glare at him, willing him to get this painful explanation over with. None of this is sounding like my golden angel is coming home to us.

"Goldie said as much last night," I tell him dismissively.

But Papa shakes his head, not in the least bit perturbed. "Robert wanted to make an independent film to be distributed by Honipot—like the deal we have with Cundall —but didn't have the funds to develop it. Cundall offered him a loan, an advance on the distribution, and he convinced his then-boyfriend to co-sign with him."

"Goldie," Baby explained, back to being enthusiastic.

"But it turned out that Goldie was responsible for the whole thing. And when the project sank after accusations of sexual assault against Robert, Goldie suddenly found himself indebted to Honipot and Cundall."

I frown. "So Goldie was already working for Honipot as well as Robert?" I try and clarify.

They both shake their heads, and Baby is practically dancing on his toes. "Goldie works in a *café*," he exclaims. "He's not trying to get into the industry. Cundall offered him a chance to work off the debt by starring in some films. It was supposed to be several, but we snapped him up. He has no intention of working with anyone else as far as Cundall knows."

My entire stomach drops through the chair and onto the floor. "He...*what?*"

I thought his nerves made sense before after the shitty way Robert talked about their sexual history. But now...

I drag my hand over my face, feeling sick.

He didn't even want to be our playmate. He was just trying to pay off a debt. Suddenly our magnificent, once-in-a-lifetime weekend together feels dirty and twisted.

"How much was the loan?" I ask in a croak, trying to focus on facts rather than feelings.

Papa's mouth turns down. "Five grand," he says grimly.

"Five?" I splutter. "Five fucking thousand pounds? That's pocket change! I'd have just *given* that to Cundall if he'd asked!"

I clench my fists so hard the nails threaten to break skin.

Baby looks between us. "He'd probably earn more than that from all the footage we took, though, right?"

"A lot more," I growl.

"Probably at least double," Papa agrees.

"Cundall fucked him over in more way than one," I say. Blood is roaring through my ears. "He never wanted to come here. He did it against his will. I treated him like a willing boy, but he was—"

Oh, fuck. I feel sick.

"No, no," Papa says urgently. He hurries around the desk and kneels at my feet, taking my hands in his. "No, Daddy. He had his safe words, but you saw it. We all did. He *shone* under your care. It was like watching a flower blossom. He loved everything we did, I know it. I'm certain. He didn't do anything against his will."

I shake my head bitterly. "But he never would have been here if Cundall hadn't put him in this position."

"But, Daddy..." Baby says hesitantly, like he wants to contradict me.

For once, I want to hear it.

I slip one of my hands from between Papa's and hold it out for Baby. He comes to me eagerly, cradling it.

"Yes, baby boy?"

He bites his lip and shakes his head. "I don't think he would have *left* if it wasn't for Cundall, either. Or Robert's invasion into our home. He kept talking about the contract. Maybe he was worried Cundall wouldn't hold up his end of the deal if he deviated from it." He sniffs and rubs his face. "Goldie was special. I honestly don't think he was here against his will, not really. And what we shared was real and magical."

I look between the two men I love so much. I was so sure, though, that having Goldie here had completed something for us, like a puzzle piece we hadn't even known had been missing.

"He kept saying it wasn't real," I say slowly.

"Maybe after everything Robert said, he was too afraid to believe it could be?" Papa suggests. "When people are outside our industry, it's easy to believe it's all just for show. They wouldn't necessarily know how to distinguish what are real emotions."

I take a deep breath, scowling as I try and process my thoughts. I worked in porn way before I met Papa and Baby. I was the one who introduced them to it. And it took people a long time to understand that we really were a genuine throuple.

"He looked so scared," I said, recalling his face just before he left. "I don't know. I just don't know what he was thinking, what he really wanted. Why didn't he just tell us about the situation, for fuck's sake? Why didn't Cundall?"

"Cundall made him swear not to," Papa says, his voice darkening. "He said he didn't want to sully Honipot's name."

I scoff. "Too fucking late for that."

"Why don't we ask him?" Baby says.

I frown at him. "Ask Cundall what? How much he'd like to be fired? A little or a whole fucking lot?"

Baby giggles. "Well, yes, that sounds good. But, no. I meant Goldie. You said you didn't know how he really felt or what he really wanted. So why don't we call him right now and *ask*? Papa got all his details from Cundall."

"No," I bark, rising to my feet. I feel my blood pumping through me for the first time since the miserable exchange this morning.

Papa also gets to his feet, looking confused. I hold both my men's hands in mine.

"You don't want to call him?" Baby asks, sounding crestfallen.

I kiss the back of his hand. "No, baby boy."

"But—" he tries to argue. My heart swells that he cares as much as I do about this, but I'm the one in charge.

It's Daddy's job to take care of *all* his men.

"I assume those details you got includes an address?" I ask Papa. His expression goes from confusion to delight.

"Yes, Daddy," he says breathlessly as Baby's mouth drops open. "It does. He's in south London."

I grin and squeeze my men's hands. "Then I say we're going on a road trip. Right now."

Baby whoops and punches the air.

I have to say I feel exactly the same way.

We're coming for you, Goldie.

16

GOLDIE

I'VE ONLY BEEN GONE THREE DAYS. HOW DO THE STAIRS UP TO my flat feel so foreign already? So alien? This doesn't seem like the real life I was determined to get back to.

In fact, it feels completely wrong compared to, say, the rolling hills of Wiltshire. Waking up to the trees rustling in the breeze and the gentle stream bubbling past my window.

I stop in front of the door to my and Mum's flat, key in hand, biting my tongue, *hard.*

I can't long for that life. I *can't.* It was all make-believe, and I don't deserve it anyway. But the entire journey home, I've been conflicted and confused. Daddy seemed so angry when I left, but that was what we'd agreed. That had been the contract.

He hadn't really expected me to stay longer, had he?

I couldn't, anyway. Not with Mum. I am glad to be back to see her and make sure she's okay. She's rubbish at remembering to respond to texts, so although I called and texted and few times, I just got quite short replies without much detail. She'd just kept insisting that she was doing great and not to worry about her.

But I *do* worry about her. All the time.

So I'm not sure why Daddy had been so surprised that I was leaving when we'd all planned for that. Sure, it was probably shitty of me to try and sneak out, but I'd been pretty certain my heart would break if we'd made a big fuss.

Instead, we'd had a fight, and Daddy had told me to fuck off. A sob catches in my chest, and I have to dig the key into my palm to stop myself from losing it completely. I always knew I wasn't going to see Daddy again—nor Papa or Baby—but the idea that they're somewhere in the world *hating* me doesn't just break my heart. It shatters it into a million pieces and stomps it all over the floor.

I know they don't love me, no matter how perfect this weekend had felt. They love *each other*. I was just a plaything they were kind to. But I wish we could have left it amicably rather than with such a bitter taste in everyone's mouths.

I still managed to find a way to ruin everything, no matter what Daddy said.

I physically shake myself. I can't lurk at the door of my own home forever. I have to step through, back into my life, as if I never met Daddy, Papa, and Baby.

Except I did, and the most important outcome is that my loan against Honipot will be written off. I have no idea how money gets made precisely in porn between paid subscribers and advertising, but with the amount of footage we managed to accumulate, there have to be several long films as well as many more short snippets and photos.

I swallow, thinking of the people who will watch it. Will they believe it looked like something more than fucking? Or will they see it as just three partners inviting someone disposable into their home for the weekend?

Enough. What's done is done. Before I can wallow any further, I jam the key into the lock and turn it, entering into our living room. Everything is just as I left it, which feels strange, considering how much has happened to me since I left.

"Is that you, darling?" Mum calls out from her bedroom, sounding strong and awake, and my heart soars.

"Hey!" I reply, dropping my keys in the bowl on the table near the door. I remove my backpack and kick off my shoes, groaning in relief. It was a pretty long journey, especially as I'd had to wait ages for my connecting train at Bath Spa because of a cancellation, and I'm aching anyway from a physically demanding weekend.

Nope, not thinking about that. *La la la.*

I walk through her bedroom door to find her not only awake but looking rosy-cheeked and smiling. She's dressed in what she calls real people clothes—in other words, not pyjamas—reading her Kindle.

"Wow, Mum," I say as I go over to give her a hug. "Did that nurse take you to a *spa?*"

She laughs and swats my shoulder as I sit down beside her. "She was excellent. And that physiotherapist worked miracles. I know I'm on an upswing right now, but I haven't felt this good for years."

I smile at her, trying to hide my sadness. If we could afford private treatment for her like this all the time, it wouldn't stop the bad periods, but it would give her so much more freedom of life when she was on the up.

As if reading my mind about money, she gives me a shrewd look. "Are you sure we were able to afford that?"

She has no idea about Robert's dodgy loan or the fact that I was dragged into it, and that's how it's going to say. So I can't admit that I used the cash I'd scrimped together to start trying to pay Mr. Cundall back on her weekend instead.

"Flora gave me a surprise bonus," I say, hoping the lie about my boss won't come back to bite me in the arse.

She beams at me and pats my knee. "She's a lovely

woman." At least that's true. Mum shakes her head and taps my knee harder. "Anyway, enough about me! How about *you?* How was your weekend? These were friends you met online, yes?"

She wasn't freaked out about that lie I'd told her at all. In fact, she'd seemed thrilled that I was going out and doing something new. Bless her. I glance at her e-reader and think about how I'd been so scared to admit to her that I read book upon book of gay romance. But as soon as I had, she'd asked for my best recommendations and become even more of a fan than I was of the genre.

She's extremely laid back about a lot of things, but I don't think I'll ever be able to tell her about this weekend, and that makes me sad. Daddy, Papa, and Baby may have been a fleeting presence in my life, but their impact will no doubt be important and long-lasting.

For better or worse.

"I had a lovely time, thank you," I say, managing a smile. Because I did. Hopefully, with time, I'll be able to remember the good parts—the *wonderful* parts—and forget the bad. "I should probably put some laundry on, though. Have you got anything for a dark wash?"

I get the feeling that Mum knows I'm slightly avoiding the question, but she doesn't push, and I'm grateful. For the next little while, I busy myself with some chores, then start working on an early dinner. A knock at the door startles us both—especially me after last night—but then Mum smiles from where she's perched on the sofa.

"Oh, that's got to be next door," she says. "They said they were popping to the shops and offered to get me a few bits."

"They're so nice," I say genuinely about the young Greek couple who moved in six months ago. They'd offered to help a few times now, and it was another reason I'd felt okay leaving Mum for the weekend. I wipe my hands on a tea towel and hurry to open the door before they have to knock again.

But it turns out I had every right to be worried.

Because yet again, Robert is standing on the other side of the door.

"WHAT THE FUCK?" I splutter in horror. He's never been to our flat before, but perhaps Mr. Cundall has given up this address as well. The thought makes me want to vomit. I *knew* that man was a creep.

I try and slam the door in his face as I hear Mum gasp behind me, but I'm not fast enough and Robert is bigger than me. He forces his way in, stumbling a bit before he pushes me back and shoves the door closed.

"I'm calling the police," I cry before realising that I've left my bloody phone in the kitchen from where I was using it as a timer to cook. I try and bolt for it, but Robert grabs my wrist and hauls me back.

"Let go of my SON!" Mum bellows. She struggles to her feet with her cane, but we all know that she'd be no match for Robert.

He sneers at her, then ignores her entirely in favour of dragging me closer to his face. He's got a spectacular shiner from where Daddy punched him last night. I smell the beer and cigarettes on his breath and flinch backwards.

"You got me fired, babe," Robert sobs. Despite my perilous situation, I feel a stab of triumph. At least something good came from all this. Daddy must have contacted Mr. Cundall today. "Why would you do that?"

I try and wriggle free from his grip. "I tried to save you from your mess!" I shout back. I've got nothing left to lose, and all the anger and distress I've been bottling up since having to leave Daddy, Papa, and Baby come bubbling to the surface. "You were the one who fucked the film up! You tried to assault my friends in their home! We're *over*, Robert! Leave me alone!"

"Robert?" Mum repeats, ice in her voice. "So you're the one who treated my son so appallingly?"

"Shut the fuck up, you *bitch!*" Robert screeches. He staggers again, and I wonder how many beers he's had. "Why did you ruin everything, babe? Why did you *whore* yourselves out to those filthy perverts? The way that man treated you was worse than an animal!"

"Daddy *cared* for me!" I bellow, not caring that I was spilling all my secrets in front of my mother. "He *treasured* me! It may have only been for a weekend, but it was better than the entire *year* we were together!"

The slap across my face catches me completely off guard. I spin and stumble into the telly, sending it crashing off its stand. Mum screams, and all I can think about is getting Robert out of here and keeping her safe. But as I manage to stagger upright again, I look up just in time to see her smack Robert across the back with her walking stick.

I gasp in shock as he goes flying, then run to Mum to help her move away from him.

"Get out of my home!" She's sobbing, brandishing the cane at him. "You leave my son alone! He's far too good for the likes of you!"

"Oh, I know he's good," Robert snarls, getting back on his feet. "I've seen the footage. He's *so* good. But he lied and was never good like that for me. He made me feel like shit, like I couldn't do anything right. So I went out to prove myself, but he ruined my film as well by fucking up the loan!"

"You're delusional!" I cry in disbelief. "You made *me* feel like shit in bed. You ruined the film *yourself* when you tried to assault one of the stars! You're *disgusting!*"

"Oh, really?" he whispers, a dangerous look in his eyes. He beings whacking knick-knacks off the sideboard and photo frames from the wall. Luckily the floor is carpeted, but then he starts picking up bits of china and hurtling them at the opposite wall so they smash.

"Stop! Stop!" Mum yells. My heart breaks for her. These are her few precious things from a life that's been pretty unfair to her, and here this brute is destroying them for no reason.

There's more banging on the door, and from the shouting, I think it's our neighbours. I hope they call the police, but I'm not sure how quickly a car could get to us.

Robert advances on Mum and shoves her down on the sofa before grabbing me around the neck. I try to hit and scratch him, but it just seems to bounce off him in his drunken rage.

I have to stop this *right now.*

"Okay! Okay!" I shout, holding my hands up in defeat. "I'll…I'll go with you. Just leave my mum alone, all right?"

"No!" Mum shouts.

Robert's victory smile is more like the bared teeth of a wild beast. He yanks me close so his mouth is pressed to my ear, his beer breath hot and repulsive against my skin.

"I'm going to take you home and defile you, you little slut," he rasps, and my stomach roils in fear and revulsion. "You like to be bossed around? Oh, I'll happily be the boss of you."

I whimper as he changes his grip to the back of my neck and starts dragging me across the living room, kicking away or stamping on any of Mum's things that gets in his way.

"NO!" Mum shouts again, even louder, but Robert just laughs cruelly.

"It's okay, Mum," I splutter. "I'll be okay!"

I'm not sure if that's true. But right now, I just have to get him out of our home and away from her. Then I just have to hope I'll have a chance to get away from him before he gets me to his house. It's several stops away by tube and on another line. If I scream for help, surely someone will intervene.

Oh…god. Unless he drove here. He does have an old banger of a car and wouldn't think twice before getting behind the wheel under the influence. If I can't get away before he gets me in the car and locks the doors…

No, I have to keep fighting! Once Mum is safe, I can scream and try and break loose to run. Maybe our neighbours really did call the police, and they're descending on the block of flats this very moment as Robert thrusts me towards the door.

He yanks it open.

On the other side is Daddy, looking furious, his fist raised just about to pound on the door.

I almost faint in relief.

17

DADDY

Papa had, rather sensibly, offered to drive us all to the
address for the flat Goldie shares with his mum. I'm less
murderous now I understand Goldie's situation much better
than before, but my thoughts are still wild, and I wouldn't
trust myself behind the wheel.

But when the doors on the lift open on Goldie's floor and
there's a couple banging on a door, shopping bags littered
around the floor, my hackles immediately rise, and I'm very
glad I'm not tired from the past couple of hours driving. The
man is talking frantically on the phone whilst the woman
continues to pound on and yell through the door.

"What's Goldie's number?" I bark as I stride down the
corridor.

"837," Papa rattles off without needing to check anything.

Of course that's the door the couple are in front of.

"That's our friend's flat," I say as the three of us hurriedly
approach. "What's wrong?"

The man on the phone (I guess to the police, from the
details he's giving) moves away so he can keep talking. The

woman pants and stops pounding to address me. "We're not sure," she says in an accent that sounds European to me but that I can't place in that moment. "But there is shouting and things breaking, and they will not open the door."

Could Goldie be fighting with his mother? I honestly have no idea what their relationship is like. But whatever is going on, my boy is inside, and I have to find out.

I raise my fist to pound in the woman's place…just as the door flies inwards.

At first, the only thing I see is the tear-stained face of my angel as his eyes alight with recognition at the sight of me. "Daddy?" he whispers.

Then I register Robert's horrified face, the trashed living room behind them, and the sobbing woman trying her best to stand up with a cane, even though she's clearly in pain.

"You let my son *go*, you fucker!" she screams, her face red and blotchy from what I imagine is pain and immense distress.

And then my thoughts pretty much stop altogether.

I don't even have to wrestle Goldie from Robert's grasp. The snivelling coward drops him immediately and uses his arms to shield his face. "Please, don't hurt me!" he squeals like a stuck pig. Except pigs are intelligent and actually quite clean, whereas this greasy fuck is neither.

I grab his collar with my left hand and lay three quick punches into his face—*one, two, three*—before spinning him around and throwing him out of yet another front door. The concerned couple jump aside in horror.

My breath is sawing through me as my vision clouds with rage. I advance on him as he scrambles backwards until he hits the wall.

"You will not contact my boy again," I say, my voice low and dangerous as I crouch down to his eye level. "You will not even think about him, is that clear? You will fuck off into the abyss, never to be heard from again, because you are a worthless piece of shit. My boy is an *angel,* and he is under my protection. So is his mother and anyone else important in his life. If you so much as *breathe* in his direction again, your life won't be worth living. Does that penetrate your thick skull?"

"Y-yes," he whimpers.

I laugh. "Yes, what?"

He blinks. "Yes…sir?"

That'll do.

"Police! Get back!"

"Oh, thank god," the man of the couple exhales as officers run down the corridor.

The woman points frantically at Robert as I back away with my hands in the air. Obviously, British police don't have guns, but I'm a big fucker, and I don't want to give them any excuses to arrest me before they understand that I'm not the instigator here.

"It was him," the woman cries, jabbing her hand at Robert. "He had our neighbour around the throat, dragging him out, until this gentleman stopped him! And I think he broke all that stuff."

The officers slow, surveying the scene. But seeing as Robert has his hands up and is crying, none of them seems to question the woman's true story, thank fuck.

"I need to check on my boyfriend. He was the one who was attacked," I tell the nearest officer, already backing into the flat. The word 'boyfriend' falls easily from my mouth. At my movement, the couple from the corridor also follow me in, along with two of the officers, presumably to see what the fuck is going on.

Baby is cradling Goldie on the floor as he sobs. Papa is comforting the woman who I assume to be Goldie's mum.

116

She looks ashen and shaky, but there's also a fire in her eyes that I immediately warm to.

I've seen that same fire in her son's eyes once or twice.

"Is that bastard gone?" she demands.

I gesture at the police. "I think he's under arrest," I assure her.

And then, unfortunately, that's all the fucks I have to give for anyone who isn't one of my boys. I sink to the floor and pull Baby and Goldie into my arms, kissing my golden angel's hair.

"It's okay, sweet boy," I tell him, rubbing Baby's back so he knows I'm looking out for him, too. "Daddy's here. You must have been so scared, but you're safe now. You were so brave. I'm so proud of you."

He takes a shuddery breath and frowns at me through his tears. For a second, I'm afraid that he's going to tell me to fuck off.

Just like I told him to fuck off this morning when I thought he didn't want us. But the way he just called me 'Daddy' has me hopeful.

However, what he asks is, "How do you know I was brave?"

I almost laugh as I kiss his forehead. "Did you protect your mum?" I ask. "Did you do everything you could to stop that arsehole from hurting her?"

His face crumples, and he starts crying again. "I just thought if I could get him away from her, then maybe I could escape before...before he...the things he said he was going to *do* to me..."

My vision threatens to white out with a rage that burns like a thousand suns.

I think I know exactly what that inhuman fuckstain had been intending to do with my precious angel.

"See?" I say, breathing evenly through my nose to try and

rein in my fury. I'm aware that Baby is watching me with wide eyes, and I need to be calm for the both of them. "Daddy knew you were brave, and now he's here to make sure you and your mum are totally okay, all right? I've got you."

"But...why?" he stammers. "I left. It was just for the weekend. Daddy...I..."

I take him by the chin, and Baby automatically grabs Goldie's hand, tight.

"Because you're *mine*, golden angel. I forgive you for being scared. I know everything now about Robert, Cundall, and the loan, and I know you were just trying to do what's right. But I'm not letting you leave again, okay? Do you understand?"

But he shakes his head. "It's not real. I know you're just being nice. You can't—"

"Goldie, I *love* you," I say forcefully, looking into his eyes. "You're mine, and I love you. Is that clear?"

Goldie just looks at me, tears pooling to the brim of his eyes.

Until Baby slams into him, throwing his arms around his waist and pressing a kiss to his cheek. "I love you, too, Goldie!" he declares.

Papa raises his hand from the sofa. "I love you as well, sweet boy, in case you were wondering."

He winks at Goldie, and the attending officer who had been taking Goldie's Mum's witness statement swivels her head between all of us. "Oh-*kay* then," she says with a nod, then turns back to her questioning.

The couple from the corridor are talking to a different officer whilst Robert is being put into handcuffs and read his rights. So I have another few minutes with my two precious boys, but my angel in particular. He's looking at me with an open mouth more appropriate to a goldfish than a golden boy.

"Did you hear us, angel?" I ask. There's a playful hint to my voice from relief. I have this crazy feeling that everything's going to be okay now.

He closes his mouth and swallows. "But...you can't," he whispers, shaking his head. "I'm not...this isn't..."

I squeeze him to me and make him look at me, that familiar calm settling in his eyes.

"Golden angel," I say, my tone carrying just a *hint* of authority. "Are you calling your Daddy a liar?"

"No, Daddy," he says immediately, his voice breathless. "No, I would never."

I smile warmly at him, my heart overflowing. Baby touches my hip and gazes longingly at our new, perfect boy.

"Good boy," I murmur to Goldie. "So if Daddy says he loves you, that's right, isn't it? You don't need to worry about anything else."

Except...fuck my fucking life...he bites his lip and looks decidedly worried. "There is one thing, though, Daddy..."

I want to tell him it doesn't matter, but I know tonight is serious. So I nod. "What is it, sweet boy?"

He's trembling, and I tighten my grip on his side, grounding him. He takes a deep breath.

"Would it...would it be very silly...totally ridiculous...if I said I loved you, too? All three of you?"

When Papa and Baby agreed to be mine all those years ago, I didn't think my heart could ever get any fuller. But right now, I know I'm the king of the world.

I press my forehead to Goldie's and squeeze Baby's hand. I want Papa with us, but I know he will be soon enough. He's my strong, handsome man, and he doesn't need me right now as much as our boys do.

119

I press a gentle kiss to Goldie's lips. "You love us?" I ask. He nods, then bites his lower lip as if to say something else.

I don't let him.

"Good," I say, touching my hand to the side of his beautiful face. "That's perfect, just the way Daddy wants it."

18

GOLDIE

I DON'T KNOW HOW LONG IT TAKES FOR THE POLICE TO TAKE all their statements and haul Robert off. I can't believe he's actually been arrested. I'm not sure he'll get much more than a slap on the wrist for being drunk and disorderly, but maybe I can get a restraining order on him or something. It just matters that the police listened to Mum and me and believed us. I wasn't sure they would.

Our neighbours insist on staying and looking after Mum, busying themselves making a round of tea for everyone. She's badly shaken up, but no harm was actually done, so she'll be okay.

With our neighbours occupied for a minute in the kitchen, it means I've got a modicum of privacy with Mum and my men.

My men, who love me.

I still can't really believe it, but Daddy's had me in his lap for the past twenty minutes, not caring what the police or our neighbours think.

It appears that the cat is somewhat out of the bag.

"So...you're the friends my son went to go visit this

weekend?" Mum asks, looking between Daddy, Papa, and Baby.

I look at Daddy, unsure what I should say. He beams at me then kisses my temple. "More than friends," he says with a possessive growl. Papa and Baby are sitting on the floor on either side of us, and they each take one of my hands. My cheeks flame at the attention, still not believing it's real.

Also...I'm not sure what my mum is going to make of it.

Sure enough, she looks between us. "What...all four of you?"

"Yes," Daddy says, gazing into my eyes, his voice warm and decisive. He's not worried about anyone judging us, but I don't want Mum to worry about me.

However, I'd momentarily forgotten that she's awesome.

"Blimey. Good for you, hun." She laughs, some of the light coming back into her eyes that Robert scared away. "You've certainly upgraded from the prick we just got arrested."

"Amen to that," Papa says darkly.

I laugh a little in relief. "You're really okay with this?" I ask her, gesturing to my three men.

She looks between us. "Are you happy, darling?"

I nod eagerly, my heart ready to burst. "*So* happy."

"Then, yes," she says with a relieved smile. "I'm delighted for you."

Our neighbours come back in with strong, sugary tea for all, and I drink it down gratefully. But my thoughts are whirring again, and I'm worried about what's going to happen next.

"How did you get here?" I ask Daddy quietly whilst the others are talking.

"We drove, angel," he says, brushing some of my hair back. "When Papa found out what Cundall had done, how he'd blackmailed you, I knew I needed you in my arms as soon as humanly possible."

He looks sad, and I touch his face, my brow furrowing in an unspoken question. He clears his throat.

"I thought...what I mean is—were you okay with everything we did together? We won't release the footage if you don't want us to. I feel like I treated you poorly, without a full understanding of the facts—"

"No, no," I say in horror, shaking my head. "I loved it, Daddy. I *loved* it. Everything was amazing. The way you take charge and make all the bad thoughts melt away is the happiest I've ever been in my life. In a way, I'm *grateful* to Mr. Cundall for his offer. I know it could have been bad with someone else, but it brought me to you three, and that never would have happened otherwise. It started out complicated, but now I feel *so* lucky."

He sighs, and I swear his eyes are misty. Then he pulls me in for a hug, and we stay like that for a while, not speaking, yet saying everything.

But I am concerned that it's getting late. "Should you drive back soon?" I ask, pulling back to look into his eyes. "Or could you get a hotel nearby?"

"Where do you live?" Mum pipes up. She's finished her tea, and now she and our neighbours each have a glass of wine, and she's looking *ten* times better than before.

"Trowbridge in Wiltshire," Daddy says with a smile. "We have a gorgeous cottage together."

"It's *so* beautiful, Mum," I say, unable to stop the wistfulness in my voice. I'd thought I wasn't going to ever see it again, but now...now I have hope.

Mum smiles at all four of us still sitting on the floor. I feel like my men have come down to my level and won't move until I'm able to get back on my feet.

"That's a fair way away," she says, frowning a little. "Will you get to see each other often?"

Daddy's grip tightens around me. "Forgive me, ma'am," he

123

says incredibly politely. "But I'll want to see your son all the time. Certainly for now I need him right next to me until I trust no more vile ex-boyfriends are going to threaten him again. I was hoping to take him home with us tonight, if that's all right with you."

"Oh, no, I can't—" I begin to splutter, but Mum takes another gulp of red wine and waves me off.

"Of course you can, darling," she insists. "You should enjoy the first throes of romance. And I'm sure after this ordeal, Flora will understand if you need to take a little time off work."

Daddy frowns. "Work? You don't need to stay at that café if you don't want to. Not now. We'll support you. Both of you," he adds with a nod to Mum.

I blink at him. Flora is nice, but the idea of no more boring shifts at the café is incredible.

"But…it's too soon," I say. "Too fast."

"You say 'too' too much," Daddy teases with a wink. "Who's in charge?"

"Daddy is," I say, blushing, aware that our neighbours are watching, fascinated. But I don't need to worry about that. I just need to let Daddy decide.

"Do you want to keep your job?" he asks.

"Not really," I admit.

He nods. "That's easy enough, then. Hand your notice in, and once we get you back to the cottage, we'll work everything else out from there."

"But Mum—" I begin.

"Will be just fine for a little while," she interrupts. "Darling, you've spent so much of your life looking after me. It's about time you started living for *yourself*. I'll find a way to manage."

Papa touches my knee. "We can arrange for private care if that would help?"

"We're pretty rich," Baby informs everyone gleefully, bouncing up and down.

I raise my eyebrows and look at Mum, who nods. "T-that —*yes*—that would help a lot," I stammer, both startled by their generous offer and not surprised at all by it at the same time.

These men are so kind.

If Mum could continue to get assistance like she had this weekend, who knows how much that would improve her quality of life.

"It sounds to me," she says with a wink, "like those are a lot of decisions that can be made later. For now, you boys should hit the road so you can make it home before midnight."

I bite my lip, glancing between her and Daddy. "Are you *sure?*"

She grins. "Go pack a bag and have some fun, my darling."

This is all so unbelievable, and it's happened so fast…but I want a relationship with these men so *badly.* If Mum really is giving her blessing…then I'd be a fool not to grab this opportunity with both hands.

I'm packed and ready to go in no time. I hug Mum and thank our neighbours, but then Daddy surprises me by also giving Mum a gentle hug.

"I'll take care of him," he promises.

"We all will," Baby chirps as he and Papa also hug her.

Mum places a hand on her heart and gives me the fondest look. "I think you've hit the jackpot here, darling."

I don't think it. I know it.

I SPEND most of the drive to Wiltshire in the back seat of Daddy's big black Jeep with Baby, holding hands and dozing.

Papa keeps Daddy company as Daddy drives, the two of them murmuring in quiet conversation as we leave London behind and head back into the countryside.

As we step through the front door, I can't quite believe I'm back in the cottage again. I only left this morning, but everything feels different now. There's a kind of electricity in the air.

Princess rubs herself against my legs in the entrance hall before slipping out the front door to go hunting. Her loud purrs stay with me, though.

"She's glad you're home," Baby says.

"We all are," Papa agrees, holding my neck and kissing the top of my head.

Daddy doesn't say anything. He just scoops me off my feet, holding me in his arms like a rag doll. I shriek and giggle as he kicks the front door closed, then carries me down the length of the house to the bedroom.

The one the public never sees.

There are no cameras as my three men take their time kissing and undressing me. Once I'm naked and feeling all floaty, they hastily undress as well, and all four of us tumble into bed.

I had been so exhausted from such a long, emotionally draining day, I'd thought I was going to pass out immediately. But there are three mouths to be kissed, and three hot, hard cocks rubbing against my skin. We all lie together, a puddle of limbs on the cool sheets, touching and moaning, whispering sweet nothings. Baby tells me how much he loves me and how pretty I am. Papa tells me what a good boy I am and that this is my home now.

But Daddy...Daddy doesn't say much with his words. He says it with how possessive his hands are cupping my face, how forceful his kisses on my mouth are, how he grinds his huge cock against my hip, leaking pre cum. But when he does speak, he just says one word:

"*Mine.*"

And finally, I think I'm ready to believe it. To stop worrying and doubting myself. This is real, and I couldn't be happier to belong to him—to all three of these incredible men.

This is the start of a new chapter in my life, and just like my favourite romance novels, I got not one but *three* loves of my life.

EPILOGUE

GOLDIE – ONE YEAR LATER

"It's just so exciting to meet you!" the lady in front of me gushes, beaming down at me and my men where we sit at our table. I'm having another pinch-me moment.

My life seems full of them these days.

But the table I'm sitting at is covered in paperback copies of my very own romance novel: *'Goldie and His Three Bears'.* I'm in America, at one of those gay romance conventions I could only ever dream of attending before as a reader. Now, I was asked to come as a *special guest,* along with my three men. We're going to be speaking on our very own panel later.

But right now, I'm signing copies of my sort-of-autobiographical novel that has sold so well, *I* was able to afford to pay for our transatlantic flights—in first class, no less.

Daddy paid for everything else, of course. But I think he knew how happy it made me to spoil my men for once. Don't get me wrong. I'm perfectly happy to be pampered most of the time, but I'm so proud of how much my life has changed in just one year.

There are a few women around our table, all clutching my book and looking at us with flushed cheeks, slightly breathless. "Y'all are even more handsome in real life," one of them titters in a southern drawl, and I beam at her.

"I know," I whisper to her conspiratorially. "How did I manage to snag not one but *three* such handsome men?"

She blushes even harder. "Your videos are just so...*ngh,*" she says, and the other middle-aged women around her giggle and blush as they nod in agreement.

I've still never watched any of the films we make, even though that first weekend had just been the first of many, *many* more. I'm proud to earn a living with my lovers, but I like to keep what we do a little magical by not watching it back. Papa understands and knows how much I respect the editing he does for us. But it's important to me that some of what we do is purely for me.

All mine, as Daddy would say.

The southern lady waves a hand and points at my and Daddy's relatively new wedding rings. "Congratulations, by the way! The photos of y'all's ceremony were just to *die* for."

It's my turn to blush and turn to look lovingly at my Daddy. In his true style, Daddy had just announced on Valentine's Day that we were going to get married, but of course I said yes, and as always absolutely loved being told what to do. Daddy knows best, after all.

Now we all have matching rings. After Daddy and I had a small legal ceremony, we then had a much bigger event for all four of us to commit to each other. I'd briefly worried that I was too young, that we were moving too fast, but Daddy knows all the best ways to stop my worrying about anything for too long.

Such, naughty, dirty, *perfect* ways.

And what do I have to worry about these days, really? I'm

a published author currently sitting at a convention with other authors I used to idolise. I'm a world-famous adult entertainer with legions of fans. I get messages daily from sweet boys like myself who say seeing me with my men make them believe that there are men out there worthy of them, too.

I have two jobs I love and three men I love even more. Daddy always says I'm greedy, and I guess I am, in the best kind of way.

I was a little concerned about allowing Daddy to pay to help Mum out, even with the best intentions. But now I have the money myself to pay for her physio and other appointments, and it feels amazing. Obviously, her MS isn't cured, and she still goes through rough patches, but she's so much better now that she's taken on a part-time job doing admin in a small office, and she loves it.

I wanted her nearby, so we all agreed to help her move out of that cramped flat in London over to Trowbridge. I don't feel like we're stepping on each other's toes, but she's close enough that I can get to her in no time if she ever needs help. I think fresh air and greenery are doing her health almost as much good as the extra medical care. Knowing she's the happiest she's ever been means I feel okay with my own incredible happiness and not guilty that I'm neglecting her.

As for Honipot, Daddy agreed not to sue Mr. Cundall for everything he's got in exchange for releasing them out of their contract with the production company. Now we distribute our films exclusively through our own website, as well as the content we put up on social media. I'm sure losing all of Daddy, Papa, and Baby's work still hurt Honipot, and I can't really feel sorry for Mr. Cundall. I might have worried about some of the other people at Honipot, but Daddy has expanded our platform to host other adult entertainers and is starting to build an empire of his own, inviting anyone who wants to switch from Honipot extra good deals.

When I'd stepped into Mr. Cundall's office a year ago, my problems had felt all too much to overcome. Then when I'd had to leave the cottage and the three men who lived in it behind, I'd felt like my life would never be enough again.

But now everything is just right, like a perfect bowl of yummy porridge. Goldie did indeed get his Three Bears.

And now they were going to live happily ever after.

———

THANK you for reading Goldie's book! Giving him and his three bears their happily ever after was such a delight to write. If you enjoyed their story, please leave a review for other readers to discover this sweet and naughty little book.

———

TURN the page to discover more of my contemporary MM fairy tale adaptations! If you loved Golden, might I suggest you start by trying Thorn in His Side, my Beauty and the Beast adaptation? Conveniently, it's available in my fairy tale box set!

———

IF YOU'D LIKE to be the first to know what fairy tale I'll be working on next, make sure to join my Facebook group, Helen's Jewels. We also have a lot of fun with games and giveaways, as well as ARC opportunities.

———

THANK YOU TO MY TEAM!

Cover Design: Cate Ashwood

Editing: Meg Cooper

Proof Reading: Tanja Ongkiehong

General Awesomeness: Pioneers (Ed and Amelia), Theodora for the butter, lovely Hubby & our magnificent fur babies.

ALSO AVAILABLE

The Fairy Tale Collection: Contemporary MM Retellings

Experience Beauty and the Beast, Cinderella, and Rapunzel as you've never seen them before in this thousand page box set of contemporary adaptations! Available together for the first time, each book is a standalone with its own HEA, but watch out for familiar faces!

THORN IN HIS SIDE

Beautiful, innocent Joshua Bellamy finds himself in an arranged marriage to the older, brutish, and scarred Darius Legrand. But in Darius's secluded mansion, Joshua begins to see that Darius isn't so scary after all. In fact, despite being a little grumpy, he's actually very protective and caring. When danger comes knocking on their door, will Joshua and Darius's blossoming love be strong enough to save each other?

A RIGHT ROYAL AFFAIR

Nobody knows that Prince James of the United Kingdom is bisexual, and as he's sixth in line to the throne, it needs to stay that way. But when he meets the cheeky, outrageously gay Essex boy, Theo Glass, everything could change. Against his better judgement, James asks Theo to help him put on a royal charity ball to remember. Can they resist their mutual attraction for a whole week alone in a picturesque castle, or will true love bloom?

HAIR OUT OF PLACE

Raphael d'Oro is a secret prince who has spent his entire life exiled in a London penthouse. But now he's in a race against time to get back to his tiny European nation to claim the throne that's rightfully his and save his people. Good thing he has his insanely hot older bodyguard to take care of him. But Griff Thompson would never want someone as inexperienced as Raphie, would he? Even *if* they keep finding themselves in places with only one bed...

eBook: *http://www.helenjuliet.com/buy/thefairytalecollection*

Audio: *http://www.helenjuliet.com/audio/thefairytalecollection*

ALSO AVAILABLE

Sweet Tooth

Getting lost in the woods was never this fun

When Hans Jager and his sister Greta have to return home for the holidays, the last thing he expects is to run into his childhood best friend, Chester Wild. Even more surprising is when Chester pretends to be Hans's boyfriend to protect Hans from his wicked step-mother's wrath. Seeing Chester again makes Hans realise that he might feel more than just friendship, but can he risk spoiling what they already have?

Chester has always loved his best friend. But Hans is straight, right? When they find themselves stranded in the woods, everything changes, but for how long? A dark family secret could undo their magical reunion, and Hans is feeling more lost than ever. Could Chester be enough to guide him back to true love?

Sweet Tooth is a steamy, standalone MM romance novel featuring a scrumptious sweet shop, slow dancing to Elton John, an explosive family dinner, a loyal puppy, a very naughty use for candy canes, and a guaranteed HEA with absolutely no cliffhanger.

Click here to get the Sweet Tooth eBook

Click here to get the Sweet Tooth audiobook

Rise and Shine

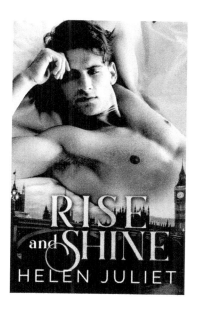

Luca feels like he's been asleep for a hundred years, but really it was just one bad night. He awakes in a room he's never seen before with a note from a mysterious stranger who seems to have come to his rescue.

Before he can sneak out, he finds himself face to face with his gorgeous knight in shining armour. It turns out that Ryan saved him from more than just a bad hangover. In a day that feels like a dream, Luca and Ryan discover their attraction, but as a simple tailor and a club bouncer, they're completely opposite. Could this really be true love?

Rise and Shine is a 17K word steamy, standalone MM romance novella featuring a match-making Labrador, too much pizza, just the right amount of sofa snuggles, and a guaranteed HEA with absolutely no cliffhanger. Please note this story was previously released as a free giveaway. No content has been changed.

Click here to get the Rise and Shine eBook

Click here to get the Rise and Shine audiobook

ABOUT THE AUTHOR

Helen Juliet is a contemporary MM romance author living in London with her husband and two balls of fluff that occasionally pretend to be cats. She began writing at an early age, later honing her craft online in the world of fanfiction on sites like Wattpad. Fifteen years and over half a million words later, she sought out original MM novels to read. By the end of 2016 she had written her first book of her own, and in 2017 she achieved her lifelong dream of becoming a fulltime author.

Helen also writes contemporary American MM romance as HJ Welch.

You can contact Helen Juliet via social media:
Newsletter (with FREE original stories) – https://www.
subscribepage.com/helenjuliet
Website – www.helenjuliet.com
Facebook Group – Helen's Jewels
Facebook Page – @helenjulietauthor
Instagram – @helenjwrites
Twitter – @helenjwrites

Printed in Great Britain
by Amazon

23239197R00081